Please return/renew this item by the
last date shown to avoid a charge.
Books may also be renewed by phone
and Internet. May not be renewed if
required by another reader.

www.libraries.barnet.gov.uk

DHONIELLE CLAYTON is the *New York Times* bestselling author of The Belles series and the co-author of the Tiny Pretty Things duology, which was adapted for a Netflix original series. She is COO of the non-profit We Need Diverse Books, and owner and co-founder of CAKE Literary.
@brownbookworm

TIFFANY D. JACKSON is the *New York Times* bestselling author of *Grown*; *Allegedly*; *Monday's Not Coming*, a Walter Dean Myers Honor Book and Coretta Scott King New Talent Award winner; and *Let Me Hear a Rhyme*.
@WriteinBK

NIC STONE is the #1 *New York Times* bestselling author of William C. Morris Award finalist *Dear Martin*, *Dear Justyce*, *Odd One Out*, *Jackpot*, and *Clean Getaway*, and the Shuri novel series with Marvel Comics.
@getnicced

ANGIE THOMAS's award-winning, acclaimed debut novel, *The Hate U Give*, is a #1 *New York Times* bestseller and major motion picture from Fox 2000. She is also the author of *On the Come Up* and *Concrete Rose*.
@angiecthomas

ASHLEY WOODFOLK worked in children's book publishing before becoming an author full-time. Her novels include the highly-acclaimed *The Beauty that Remains* and *When You Were Everything*.
@ashwrites

NICOLA YOON is the #1 *New York Times* bestselling author of *Instructions for Dancing*; *Everything, Everything*; and *The Sun Is Also a Star*. She is a National Book Award finalist, a Michael L. Printz Honor Book recipient, and a Coretta Scott King New Talent Award winner. Two of her novels have been made into major motion pictures. She's also co-publisher of Joy Revolution, a Penguin Random House young adult imprint dedicated to love stories starring people of colour.
@nicolayoon

BLACKOUT

Dhonielle CLAYTON

Tiffany D. JACKSON

Nic STONE

Angie THOMAS

Ashley WOODFOLK

Nicola YOON

First published in the USA by Quill Tree Books, part of HarperCollins Children's Books, a division of HarperCollins*Publishers*, 195 Broadway, New York, NY 10007

Published in Great Britain 2021 by Electric Monkey, part of Farshore
An imprint of HarperCollins*Publishers*
1 London Bridge Street, London SE1 9GF

farshore.co.uk

HarperCollins*Publishers*
1st Floor, Watermarque Building, Ringsend Road, Dublin 4, Ireland

ISBN 978 0 7555 0306 3
Printed in Great Britain by CPI Group
1

A CIP catalogue record for this title is available from the British Library

Typeset by Avon DataSet Ltd, Arden Court, Alcester, Warwickshire B49 5HN

MIX
Paper from
responsible sources
FSC™ C007454

To Black kids everywhere:
your stories, your joy, your love, and your lives matter.
You are a light in the dark.

THE LONG WALK
ACT 1

Tiffany D. Jackson

Harlem, 5:12 p.m.

It's a heatstroke kind of day. One where bad stuff happens. Tensions matching the temperature makes people do stupid things in a city full of millions. On days like this, you wouldn't catch me dead outside. I'd be huddled in my room, next to the air conditioner, streaming movies, with an iced tea and a turkey on wheat. So when the train doors open on the hot-ass platform, blowing sticky air in my face, I have second thoughts about the new job.

Out of the station, I'm surprised to see so many people on the street, the Apollo Theater's sign gleaming in the brutal sun. If this was my film set, we'd be wrapped, or I'd switch to night shoots. Concrete melts the bottom of my sneakers as I run down 125th Street, train delays setting me back a whole ten minutes. The MTA doesn't give a damn about being on time, even during a heat wave. Now I'm going to be late. Well, I'll be on time but that's the same as being late! Dad always says, *If you're early, you're on time; if you're on time, you're late.*

That's why I never chilled in the halls between classes, was always first in my seat minutes before the second bell would ring. Think that's why all the teachers liked me. It showed I respected them. Even Mr. Bishop, and no one hated gym more than me.

My dress is soaked by the time I take the elevator up to the fourth floor. I don't think I've ever sweat this much in my entire life. But they said I needed to drop off my paperwork before Monday's training.

Yes, HR orientation training. For a legit job. Your girl is the new office assistant at the Apollo corporate headquarters. My advisor hipped me to the opening. Working for the most famous Black theater in New York, known for the start of such music superstars like Michael Jackson, Mariah Carey, and Stevie Wonder, will have me kiki-ing with elite celebrities. Good practice for when I become a big-time director.

The pay: $3,500 for six weeks.

Sure, it's all the way in Harlem, no less than an hour and change by train from Brooklyn. But it puts plenty of distance between Bed-Stuy and me all summer long.

I don't want to be around there anymore. Not since . . . it happened. Not since "we" became a him and her, then a me.

The acceptance email said to arrive at five fifteen, and since this was going to be the first time my coworkers would see me, I put on my new yellow-and-blue baby doll dress, bought thanks to some graduation funds. You know what? I'm going to buy a whole new wardrobe before school, all to match my new life as

I leave my old one behind. Might even start introducing myself as Tam instead of Tammi. *Who would know the truth?* It's not like anyone's coming down to Clark Atlanta with me. I'll be there . . . alone.

It wasn't supposed to be like this, I think as I approach the reception desk. "We" had different plans. Promises made. But there's no longer a *we*, and it's time I learn how to live my life without him.

"Hey, hon." The elderly Black woman beams, sweat dripping off her brows. "Can I help you?"

I pull back my shoulders and shake the thoughts away. "Hi, my name is Tam Wright. I'm the new intern, here to drop off my paperwork."

"All right, then. Let me see if Maureen is here to sign off. Whew, hot enough for you?"

The windowless office area is steamy. I peep men and women at their desks in damp clothes. "Um, yeah."

She turns to grab a folder off the desk. "Well, heard it hit 101 around noon and hasn't come down since."

I wrap my braids up in a high bun, fanning my face.

"Is it always this hot in here?" I'm trying not to panic but I'm already thinking about the few dresses and shirts I own that'll keep me cool in here all summer. I need everything to look perfect. Everything needs to be perfect.

She throws me a sympathetic smile. "Sorry, love, system has been acting up all day. I think a –"

"Whewwww! Shit. Sorry I'm late!" The voice behind me

makes me jolt and stiffen, my skin going cold, even inside this oven. I close my eyes and start to pray.

Please don't let it be him. Please, God. Please. Anyone but him.

"Hey, hon. Can I help you?" the woman asks.

His hard steps sound like the killer approaching. He always wore sneakers that were either too big for him or that he refused to lace, soles slapping the floor, giving a high-five with each stride.

"Hey! How you doing, I'm Kareem . . ." His voice trails off until he yells, "Tammi?"

Damn.

I finally open my eyes and pivot to face him. That brown skin. Those beautiful eyes. It's not like I haven't seen him. We're neighbors and went to the same school, Stacey Abrams Preparatory, on the Upper West Side. But this is the closest I've stood near him in the last four months – close enough to smell, and I wish he didn't smell so damn good.

"What are you doing here?" I ask. It comes out real aggressive but with good reason.

He rolls his eyes, turning to the receptionist as if I were a ghost. "Sorry about that. I'm here to drop off some paperwork for orientation."

Orientation? No, no, no . . . we can't work at the same place. No way!

"Wait, you're both here to drop off paperwork?" she asks.

"No," we say in unison and glare at each other.

"I mean, yes," we say in unison, again.

4

Mortified, I take a step to widen the space between us and clear my throat.

"What I mean to say is, *I'm* here with my paperwork. I don't know what *he's* doing here."

He grins. "Guess I'm here for the same reason."

Her eyes toggle between us, and she quickly opens the folder in her hand, scanning papers. She returns to her computer screen, reading something hard while I steal a quick glimpse of him. He's wearing his favorite jeans (even in this heat), a black polo shirt, and a fresh pair of Jordans. Probably ones *she* made him get. Kinda miss his beat-up red Converse and collection of superhero T-shirts.

Stop it, Tammi! You don't miss anything about this dummy.

"Uhhh, just a second," the receptionist says, her voice shaky. "You two can have a seat. I'll be right back with Maureen."

Kareem and I exchange a suspicious glare as we slowly head over to the waiting area. Hopefully Maureen won't take too long to come get me . . . and leave his ass here.

I sit on one side of the entrance door while Kareem sits on the opposite, fidgeting.

Just keep it cute, Tammi.

I do a quick selfie-check, making sure all that heat I trekked through hasn't melted my edge control. I don't want him, but I don't want him seeing me looking a mess either.

"Whoa," Kareem mumbles to himself, staring up at something, and I follow his eyes.

"Whoa," I gasp. The walls of the waiting area are a mural of old Apollo concert posters. James Brown, Ray Charles, Ella Fitzgerald, Billie Holiday – people my grandparents grew up listening to. I didn't notice any of this before and it hits me – I'm within the very same halls these legends walked through. The warmth of that thought makes me almost forget about the jerk on the other side of the room. Is this what it's going to feel like when I'm in TV studios and on film lots?

Kareem is still fidgeting, digging through every pocket he has. Does that when he's flustered or running late, which is almost always. He wouldn't have made it to school at all if *I* hadn't set several alarms on his phone for him. Wonder if he still has them.

Kareem slaps his forehead, cursing under his breath. He must have forgotten something –

Stop it! Stop thinking about him. He's not thinking about you.

What is he even doing here? Mr. Taylor, our guidance counselor, told me about this position but said there would be only one opening, for one student interested in studying media and entertainment. Kareem said he wanted to major in boring business accounting so he could learn how to "count all his stacks." Oh, that's it! The money; he wants that $3,500.

Well, too bad for him, I'm the real deal here. I even sent my film reel with the application (all shot and edited on my phone). This job is mine! Plus . . . I need this. It's one more step on the road to a star on the Hollywood Walk of Fame. Mom and Daddy still aren't totally on board with my plan.

Only Kareem was. And now . . . he probably couldn't care less. So I won't let him take this away from me. He might as well dip and catch that A train back to Brooklyn.

I whip out my phone, trying to find something to focus on so I don't keep stealing glances at him. He hasn't changed much. Still tall as hell, all legs and gangly arms with those beautiful eyes and thick lips. He looks a little browner. Maybe he's been to the beach . . . with her. The thought makes me ill. I can imagine them trekking out to Far Rockaway, her in a skimpy bikini, him bare-chested–

"Hey, you got a charger?"

It takes a moment for it to register that he's talking to me.

"What?" I cough out.

"A charger," he says all slow like I can't speak English. "I forgot to charge up and I'm on, like, five percent."

I blink in sheer disbelief. "Is . . . is that all you got to say to me?"

He frowns. "What you mean?"

As usual, he's freaking clueless.

"You haven't said more than two words to me in months and the first ones out your mouth is you asking for something."

At first, he's just stunned. But then his eyes narrow, and he's leaning back in his chair, sucking his teeth.

"Never mind," he snaps, crossing his arms. "Don't even know why I bothered. You only care about yourself."

"What's that supposed to mean?"

"Nothing," he grumbles.

I glance up at the receptionist, now back at her desk, and she averts her eyes, pretending not to be listening. His phone wouldn't be dying all the time if he wasn't using it like a DJ speaker. Even if I did have a charger, I wouldn't give it to him. Not if he was the last boy on earth. I'll stay petty AF forever.

He sucks his teeth again, slouching further in his seat. "Man, you acting like I'm asking for a twenty. Cheap-ass."

"Yo, you done? Or are you gonna mumble some more shit under your stank breath?"

Kareem's eyes narrow, ready to kill.

"Hello there!"

We both jump to our feet at the singsong voice of a woman who is rounding the reception desk, heading straight for us.

"Hi! I'm Maureen. You must be Tammi Wright. And you, Kareem Murphy?"

"Yeah," we say in unison and I hate myself for loving the way we sound together.

Get it out of your head, girl! There is no "we." We is gone, dead. Forever.

She shakes both our hands then sighs. "Well, hate to say this, but I wish we were meeting on better terms."

"What do you mean?" we both ask, and I hold in a groan.

"This is pretty embarrassing. There's been a small clerical error. It appears an offer letter for the internship was sent to both of you. But, unfortunately, we only have the budget to cover one opening."

My stomach tenses, jaw tightens.

Kareem crosses his arms, brows making a deep V. "So what does that mean?"

She visibly gulps. "Only one of you got the position."

Kareem and I share a glance, then *click*, the room goes black. Just like that.

One minute I'm staring up into those beautiful brown eyes I've missed, and the next . . . nothing. Not a smooth FADE TO BLACK, DISSOLVE, or CUT TO. The movie just ends.

Confused, I reel back as voices rise out of the shadows.

"What the hell!"

"What's happening?"

"Everyone stay calm!"

In the rise of panic, there are footsteps and screeching chairs. Maybe someone hit a light switch by accident, but they would've turned it back on by now. Something's wrong. Where's Kareem?

"Hey! What's going on?" I shout, waving my hands in front of me, eyes trying to adjust to the dark. Something bumps into me hard and I shriek.

"Tammi?" His voice sounds far away, mixed in the chaos.

"Kareem," I want to yell back, but the name is stuck in my throat.

Phone flashlights ignite, like a scattering of spotlights. Then there's another *click*. Lights, but not as bright as before. Emergency lights, one every ten feet or so, leaving most of the office still in darkness. Across the waiting area, Kareem spins around, locking eyes on me, and I'm not entirely sure, but I could've sworn he looked almost relieved. Office doors open; dim daylight seeps in from a few narrow windows facing a brick building.

After five minutes of scrambling, Maureen shouts, "Everyone, we're evacuating!"

"Are you sure?" the receptionist asks.

"Old building. Not sure how long the generator will hold up. Everyone outside! Use your flashlights and take the stairs."

Kareem and I say nothing as we follow the crowd out the door and down the hall toward a bright red exit sign.

There are more people in the stairwell, the whole building taking the same route. My heart starts to hammer.

Maybe it's some type of fire drill or someone burned their lunch.

Outside, the streets are crowded with people pouring out of every building. They cover the sidewalks, all on their phones in collective confusion. In the mix of heat, humidity, panicky voices, and blinding sunlight, my breath catches. Something's happening.

"What's going on?" I ask a man on the corner near the train station. "Are we . . . being attacked or something?"

Even asking the question makes me want to vomit.

"Some type of power outage," the man says, scrolling through his phone. "Affecting the whole city."

"What? The whole city?" Kareem asks. Didn't even notice him still behind me.

I fish out my phone and call Mom. She answers on the second ring.

"Are you okay?" she asks, and I can hear my older brother and sister arguing in the background.

"Yeah. I'm fine. The power is out here."

"Yeah, here too. Where are you?"

"I'm outside the Apollo . . . with Kareem."

She gasps. "He's there . . . with you?"

"Yeah. I'll, uh, explain later."

"Wowwww. Okay. Come home as soon as you can."

"I will. See you soon."

"Be safe, Tammi."

I text my dad and let him know I'm okay. His tour bus is probably stuck in traffic somewhere now. And no idea where my little brother, Tremaine, is. Probably somewhere snapping pictures. At least I know he can take care of himself. More people pile into the street. My family is safe, but am I? Doesn't look like anyone has a clue what's going on or why the power's out. The city could be under attack and no one would even know it!

"Hey," Kareem says. I almost forgot he was standing next to me. "Uh, can I see your phone?"

"Why?" I snap.

"Mine's almost dead and I need to call my moms."

I slap the phone in his hand. "Go ahead."

He shakes his head and dials a number. He really didn't have to. His mom is still saved in my contacts.

"Nah, Ma. It's me," he says. "Yeah. Yeah, long story. Anyway, power out there? It is? Damn, here too. Okay, I'm on my way. Yeah, I know, Imma try. Aight? See you soon."

He clicks off and hands the phone back. "Thanks for sparing your free minutes."

I want to knock the sarcasm out his mouth until I spot Maureen.

"Oh, hey! Ms. Maureen!" We push through the crowd in her direction as she stands by the curb.

"Guys, sorry, now's not a good time; I'm taking a head count," she says without looking at us. "You two should go home. We don't know how long this is going to last. Come back on Monday, okay?"

"But," I start, "you never told us who got the position. Which one of us should come back?"

"This really isn't a good time," she says, flustered. "I'm sorry, but right now, I have to make sure everyone is accounted for. It's protocol. Once the power is back up, I'll let you two know, okay? Get home safe!"

She walks off quick before I have time to stop her.

"I can't believe this," I say, throwing my hands up. "We have to wait the entire weekend?"

"Think we got bigger things to worry about," Kareem says, holding out his hand. "Lemme see your phone again."

"For what now?"

"Yo, we in middle of an emergency and you being *this* difficult?"

"Ugh! Fine! Just don't use up all the power."

He checks his phone to look up a number before dialing. "Ay yo, Twig, what's good, fam? Nah, calling on my . . . friend's phone. My phone straight up dead, T."

Twig is one of our neighbors from the block. Tall, thin, and gangly like a baby tree. Why was he calling him? What was so important he'd waste battery life for?

"Yeah, the power is out all over the damn city. It's crazy," he says. "But what's good for tonight? Yeah? You for real? Aight, bet. See you soon."

He hands back my phone and digs out his wallet. "How much money you got?"

"Why?"

He huffs, waving at the station ahead. "'Cause if there's no power, it means there's no trains either. We need to get a cab."

Damn, he's right. The trains will be down, and I definitely don't want to be caught in them tunnels in the dark.

He counts the cash in his wallet. "I got twenty. You?"

I only have five dollars.

"That ain't gonna be enough to get us back home," he says. "With the stoplights out, we'd be lucky if this gets us ten blocks."

"Um, there's a bank across the street," I offer. "I can use my debit card."

"Power out means ATMs are out too."

"Shit," I mumble. "What do we do?"

I don't know why I asked him. Probably because there's no one else around and I'm trying to keep calm despite the growing panic in my chest.

He looks up at the street sign and takes a deep breath. "Aight. Let's do this."

He starts walking away and I follow.

"Where are you going?"

"Home. Where else?"

"But how?"

He shrugs. "Walk."

"Walk! From here?"

"You got any better ideas?"

"That's, like, mad far! It'll take you days."

He scowls. "Quit playing. Ain't like we in the Bronx."

I look up at the street sign. He wants to walk from 125th Street back to Brooklyn? We might as well be in the Bronx.

"Welp," I say with a wave. "Later, then."

"What you mean? You coming with me."

"Pssh! The hell I am!"

"Look, we don't know how long this thing is going to last, but I'm not waiting to find out. It's after five thirty. I ain't trying to get caught out here after dark. You ain't got no money, the ride apps are surging, and I ain't got no phone. So we gonna have to stick together 'til we make it home. Then you can go back to hating me or whatever."

Hey, I never said I hated him! Well, out loud.

Glancing around, I weigh my options. Maybe the power won't be out for that long. Maybe it'll just be a few more minutes, two hours tops. But what if he's right? What if it takes all night to fix and we're stuck here?

"We'll take Frederick Douglass down to Central Park West," he says.

MTA workers tape off the station entrance. Wonder how many people are stuck down there in the dark . . . with the rats? Just the thought makes my hands tremble. But there are worse things . . . one in particular that I'm desperate to avoid.

"You coming or nah?" Kareem snaps.

I sigh at the setting sun and take the first step in his direction.

MASK OFF

Nic Stone

A subway car, 5:26 p.m.

Tremaine Wright isn't a fan of enclosed spaces. A fact that *I*, Jacorey "JJ" Harding, Jr., only know because six years ago in sixth grade, a group of my goon-ass friends chased Tremaine through the boys' locker room and shoved him into the tiny custodian's closet.

So dude's in there and he's pounding and shouting, "Let me out, man! This ain't funny!" And while I wasn't one of the fools standing against the door to hold him in, I knew my half-assed "Come on, y'all. Let the mans out," didn't have enough gas for them to take me seriously . . . Not my proudest moment, but it's whatever.

The bell rang, and we all jetted.

I wouldn't have thought anything of it if Tremaine had showed up a few minutes late to our next class like I expected him to. *No harm, no foul*, my young (dumb) self thought.

But he didn't.

Clock ticked on. Tremaine's seat stayed empty. And I

remember looking around the room in a daze, like, wondering if anybody *else* noticed that homie's tardy had morphed into a straight-up absence. Which is when I started getting nervous. What if something happened to him? What if, worse (in my twelve-year-old mind at least), he snitched on the group and included me as a culprit? Probably my guilty conscience yacking at me for not *actually* being helpful to the dude, but your boy was shook, is what I'm saying. I could feel the sweat beading up at my hairline and dripping down my sides from what would soon be funky armpits. What if I got in trouble? If I did, my pops wouldn't let me hoop. He'd said as much at the beginning of the school year.

Halfway through the class period, I couldn't take it no more. Asked to be excused to the bathroom. Took everything in me not to *run* back to the locker room. Walking past the toilet stalls and the showers to that custodial closet was like the longest, scariest fifteen seconds of my young life, swear to God. Wasn't a single sound coming from the other side of the door. Which to my horror-movie-loving ass meant he was (1) gone and probably telling on us at that very moment, or (2) gone and not coming back . . . aka dead. As a doornail, or whatever they say.

I'm the one who screamed when I pulled the door open and found him sitting between a tower of giant toilet paper rolls and one of those big yellow rolling mop buckets - full of water the color of gargoyle snot.

Craziest part? He didn't even look up. Just kept staring

straight ahead into what must have been some sorta *great beyond* abyss or something.

"Uhhh . . . Tremaine?" I dropped down and put a hand on his shoulder. "Tremaine!" Gave him a shake. He snapped out of it and turned to me.

And *that's* when he screamed. And knocked the TP tower down. Then just sat there breathing mad hard.

I peeked over my shoulder. Scared. "Yo, you good, man?" Great, homie was alive, but getting caught in *here* when we were supposed to be in class wasn't a good look. "We umm . . . kinda need to get outta this closet . . ."

He looked at me in this sorta weird way . . . like confused, but also a little bit sad with a dash of surprise on top? Hard to describe.

Then he nodded. "Don't really like enclosed spaces," he said. Mad flat.

"Cool. Let's exit this one." I stood and extended a hand. He took it. Climbed to his feet.

He looked around at the scattered toilet paper rolls. "Should we, uhhh–"

"Nah, nah," I said. "They won't know it was us. Let's just go."

He nodded, and we left the locker room in silence, but as soon as we passed the half-court line in the gym, he said, "Umm . . . so can we maybe not tell anybody about this?"

"Huh?"

"The whole . . . *claustrophobia* thing. I know your guys like to mess with me or whatever, but I'd prefer if they didn't have anything extra to use."

"Oh." Made sense. "Yeah, of course." And then that guilt over not doing more started creeping on me. Making my throat itch. "I'm uhh . . . sorry I didn't stop them." (And at the same time, my ass was hoping he'd never tell anybody I said that. Just terrible.)

"I heard you tell them to leave me alone," he said. Which shocked the hell outta me, let me tell you.

"Oh."

"Could you have tried harder? Yeah." He looked at me then. "But at least you came back to get me." And he smiled. I swear I could see his whole set of braces. They alternated blue and green. I quickly looked away because him grinning at me like that made my face feel kinda hot.

Shit was uncomfortable, though I wasn't exactly sure why.

"I do appreciate that part," he said.

"It's cool, man. Don't mention it. I'll umm . . . I'll try to be firmer if they bother you again."

"That'd be nice," he said.

And that was it. We broke apart at the front office since he needed to scoop a tardy slip, and I continued back to class with the pass I used to leave.

Zero acknowledgment when he finally did enter the classroom - from me or him.

I kept my word and told my guys to lay off. And they did. But between Tremaine and me? Not a word (that *he* knows of at least) in the almost six years since that incident.

Zero acknowledgment.

Right now, though? On this dark-ass train? Tremaine Wright is the only thing I can see.

It's been a little over four minutes since all the lights went out and the train slowed to a stop. We're on the A headed to Brooklyn. I got on at my regular stop - 145th, literally three blocks from our apartment. Then at the 125th Street stop, the doors slid open, and Tremaine stepped on.

My first thought was *What the heck is Tremaine Wright doing in this neighborhood when school is out?* But then I noticed that he's got his trusty camera with him, so I figured maybe he was taking pictures or something. Homie's been on the yearbook staff since eighth grade. Always got some kinda camera on him.

The car we're on is full but not packed to the brim – seats are all taken and there's a smattering of folks standing here and there: lady pushing a stroller; hipster-lookin' bearded dude with his bike; trio of girls in ballet clothes who couldn't be more than thirteen; pair of guys who I *assume* are a couple based on how close together they're standing.

However, despite it not being too jammed, it's enough people on here for that initial simultaneous *Gasp!* when it went dark to make me feel like all the air was being sucked out the universe.

Within seconds, the conductor's bored-sounding voice crackled over the intercom talkin' 'bout "mechanical difficulties."

Held breath quickly turned to a collective huff. Mumbling. Grumbling. Sucked teeth.

And then the cell phone flashlights started coming on.

It was eerie as hell at first, but after a few minutes, once my eyes adjusted, I relaxed a little bit. Enough, even, to look in Tremaine's direction.

Both of the people beside him and the three folks sitting across the aisle have their phone lights on, so despite him being in shadow, I can see him pretty clearly. When he first got on, I tried not to think about whether or not *he* saw *me* – so of course that's *all* I could think about – but right now he's got his head leaned back against one of them IF YOU SEE SOMETHING, SAY SOMETHING posters. And his eyes are closed.

I'd almost say he looks mad relaxed, but every few seconds – and yeah, I do watch long enough to notice – he pokes his lips out like he's about to whistle. Then his mouth closes again.

I look at his chest to see if I can tell when it's rising, and as I do, I'm thrown back to a moment I must've stuffed deep down somewhere nobody could ever find it – myself included:

Starts with me. Last year. I was the only sophomore to start varsity, an honor I wore around like an invisible *S* on my chest. Couldn't tell me *nothin'*. That is until game four when I went in for a smooooooth lay-up, got fouled, and came down real funky on my right ankle. Major sprain. Never felt pain like that in my life.

I'm sitting on the ground, eyes squeezed shut, hugging my knee to my chest. Scared out my skull, but not wanting to let it show, because according to every coach I've ever had, *Real men never show fear.* Trainer is talking all calm: "Breathe in through the nose . . . *mmhmm*, that's it. Now purse your lips, and out through the mouth. You got it." Then when she gave the word, a couple of the senior guys came over to help me up so I could *hop* my deflated-ego-havin' ass to the locker room. When I was on my feet, I happened to look into the crowd. And who did I lock eyes with?

Tremaine Wright.

He was standing in the bleachers, a few rows up from the floor. Bulky camera in hand. Just staring at me. All . . . concerned.

Intercom crackles on the train: "All right, folks, word from up top is city's experiencing a blackout. Not a whole lot we can do 'cause all the signals are down. So sit tight, and I'll update you as soon as I know something."

Another round of mumbling. Grumbling. Sucked teeth.

Settling in.

Except for Tremaine. Homie's chest is definitely expanding and contracting real heavy right now. Taking deep breaths, I assume.

And his leg is bouncing like crazy. Like a video game controller during a mad intense round of Call of Duty. Not sure I realized a leg *could* bounce that fast.

My eyes drop to his foot – without my express permission, mind you – and when I see his utterly pristine white-on-white-on-white Jordan Retro 1s (*so* pristine, they practically glow on this dark-ass train), I look away.

Quick inventory: the two dudes are now sitting on the floor looking at something on one of their phones with heads literally together (gotta be a couple). Trio of dancer kids are huddled in a clump, looking like they wish their parents were here. Bike dude has turned his headlight thing on and aimed it at the ceiling. Looks real proud of himself for having the idea.

The baby in the stroller starts crying at the opposite end of the train, and my head turns (even though nobody else's does – #NewYork). The moms has her cell phone lying flashlight-up on the top of the stroller, so I can see her swoop down and scoop up the little homie. Then quick as a flash, she's got a boob out, and the kid is getting its grub on.

It makes me smile. At least *one* person on this joint won't have a growling stomach. And real talk, I admire this mom for not covering herself up or whatever. Like fine, it's dark as hell and nobody can *really* see anything, but still. I personally don't think a mom should *have* to cover the baby when he's – or *she*'s, or . . . they're – eating.

Not that I would say that shit out loud.

I shake my head.

Of *all* the times for there to be a blackout. Not only am I stuck inside this damn tin can with Tremaine for the foreseeable future, tonight was supposed to be a fresh start. End of basketball season was rough – lost my mojo for a minute – but ya boy was on *fire* during this whole first week of summer training camp.

Teammates been gassing me up. I'm feeling like a new me.

And more than that, Langston's cousin – Kayla's her name and she's visiting from down south somewhere – saw a picture of me with Lang and apparently took a liking. I'm typically not one to entertain even the *idea* of interacting with the family member of a teammate beyond a certain level (read: saying whassup if I see them in the hallway). But Lang is the one who told me she was feelin' me. *And* she's gorgeous.

So.

When I got that DM asking if I'd come kick it with her at this party in Brooklyn tonight, I said yes. Told Lang I'd come through and help him pick his 'fit and all that, and figured if I left early enough, I could also pop in on my granddad (gotta love living in Harlem – basically the opposite end of the city from where all the stuff *I'm* interested in goes down). It's why I'm on this train in the first place: New season, new girl, new start. New me.

Well . . . as far as anybody *else* knows, *Old* me. Ball me: JJ "Jump-Jump" Harding. (And though the "JJ" is technically for "Jacorey Jr.," it works real nice, don't it?)

Would I ever tell anybody I'm not really *feelin'* the hoop life no more? That where basketball used to be the light of my path/ my reason for being/the only thing I looked forward to, it's just kind of . . . a *thing* now? Maybe even a slightly tedious one?

No sooner than I'd tell 'em I think women should be able to nurse without a cloth cover joint making the baby all hot.

Speaking of hot, might just be me, but this train car is starting to feel a tad toasty.

Now *I* take a deep breath. Sneak another peek at Tremaine. His eyes are still closed, and his hardcore deliberate breathing is still evident, but both of his legs are going now. Alternating like a pair of sticks in the thick of a drumroll. I kinda wanna check on him, but after what happened a couple months ago . . . man, I don't know.

My guess is he was headed to the same party as me. The DJ is his older sister's ex-boyfriend after all, and I've heard Tremaine takes all the "in-action" pics for homie's website and gets paid pretty well to do so. (I mean, why *else* would someone follow a sibling's ex around with a camera?)

I peek back at them white-on-white-on-white J's before shutting my own eyes and letting my head fall back against the rail map behind me. Honestly feels like self-desecration considering the fresh cut I got this afternoon. Tempted to hold my *own* cell phone flashlight up and aim it at my head so people can at least see the wonders my barber works.

I think about Tremaine's chest and try to match my breathing to the rhythm I just saw in his.

In through the nose. Out through the mouth.

His shoes fill my head.

At some point, I'm gonna hafta stop keeping everything quiet.

Twelve minutes down.

I lied before.

That whole "zero acknowledgment" thing?

Yeah . . . it's not true. At all.

I've always wanted it to be, but if Imma be honest – and that's all I *can* be on this dark train with nothing keeping me company but the thoughts I usually drown out with Shit-To-Do – since that day in our middle school locker room all them years ago, "zero acknowledgment" has been impossible.

And I kinda hate it. Not only because I know, and have always known, what it "means" (though admitting it to anyone – myself included – is a bridge I haven't crossed yet), but also because I'm not the only one *acknowledging* the guy. Homie could scoop just about anybody he wanted. Like . . . across the *gender spectrum*, as my baby sister, Jordy, refers to it.

I can't say for *sure* because I never let myself get close enough to him to confirm, but I think we're about the same height. Both six three-ish. He might even have me by an inch or so.

Homie ain't no lanky joint either. That's the wild part. He's as cut as half my teammates. That's one of the things that bugs me out, honestly. Ain't nobody saying it aloud, but we all know people expect dudes like me and Tremaine – tall, "athletic"-looking fellas of a certain racial demographic (I'm rolling my eyes real hard right now) – to be athletes. Hoop. Have "hands" conducive to throwing and catching different types of "sports balls" (another one from the baby sis). Hell, I was four the first time my pops put a basketball in my hands.

But Tremaine has always seemed so unfazed about the whole *expectations* thing. I remember being in the hall at school once and overhearing one of my asshole teammates say, "Tragic that a mans with your height and build would rather handle a camera than a rock" (as in the orange-and-black sphere central to my sport of choice).

It caught me off guard how much I wanted to punch the guy, but Tremaine just smiled and said, "Somebody's gotta snap the image for that future poster of yours, bro."

Clown-ass teammate couldn't even come up with a response. Just stood there with his mouth all open, lookin' like he'd witnessed something supernatural.

I thought about that shit for *weeks*.

I dunno. There's a part of me that wishes I could be as . . . settled as Tremaine seems to be. Comfortable *as himself* or however you wanna put it. It's crazy to me that I'm one of the top ten high school hoopers in the state, and I constantly feel like none of it is legit. Like any minute somebody is gonna find out about the *real* me. Then I bug out wondering why that would be a problem.

Tremaine, though? People be saying all *kinda* wild shit about dude – there are rumors he "deflowered" both the starting quarterback *and* his girl – but it never seems to bother him. It's just him and his camera. Dude is always mad clean (like, wardrobe is immaculate) and cool as a cucumber. Documenting shit.

Usually.

Right now, his chest is moving up and down a little faster than it was before, and as corny as it makes me feel, I'm getting worried.

The urge to go over there and check on him is amping up . . .

But I haven't had any *real* contact with dude in years. What would I look like going up to him on a dark train, during a blackout, acting all *concerned* like we friends or something?

Bruh would look at me eight versions of sideways.

Wouldn't he?

Yeah, I half-assed my "allyship," as Jordy refers to it, and went back to help him in sixth grade. And yeah, *if* he still has the claustrophobia thing, there's a chance he's flippin' out inside right now, trapped in this narrow-ass subway car.

But what if I'm wrong?

What if he's mad I haven't really said nothing to him since middle school?

What if he gets the wrong idea?

His Day-Glo bright white kicks draw my eye again.

What if he gets the *right* one?

Eighteen minutes.

Folks are getting restless.

The dude couple is definitely a *couple* couple. One dude is holding the other one, who has his eyes closed. Kinda reminds me of the way Langston's dads sit all close together at our games, cheering their boy on like it's the most normal thing ever. Which . . . it basically is, ain't it? My folks come to our games and be all up on each other. Why wouldn't Lang's?

Why am I struggling so much with this shit?

Anyway, hipster bike homie is now sitting *on* his two-

29

wheeled steed, feet on pedals, looking like he's ready to ride out this joint the second the doors open.

Ballet girls are huddled together.

Baby is knocked out (I assume) in the stroller, but mom-dukes looks mad frazzled, moving the thing back and forth like *she'll* burst into tears if she stops.

And Tremaine . . . well, I haven't been able to lift my eyes past his feet.

I wish there was cell service in this tunnel. Something else about my baby sis: she knows stuff about me that no one else does. Just off intuition. I haven't confirmed or denied any of her speculations, but lately she been dropping these hints that let me know she's got some *ideas* about me. Like back in March, she was all asking me about my "prom plans":

Her: "So what's the move, big bro?"

Me: "What you mean, like what girl Imma ask?"

Her: (with a shrug) "Or guy. We're two decades into the twenty-first century after all."

April, she randomly accosted me on one of the rare occasions we were both doing homework at the kitchen table: "You know something, JJ?" she said, peeping over the top of the Malcolm X-ish glasses she rocks. "I'm really looking forward to the day you bring home a beloved." (What fourteen-year-old even speaks like that?)

"Jordy, are you talking about?" I said.

"I just think you'll make an excellent romantic partner to someone."

"Aka you want me to get a girlfriend?"

She shrugged. (This girl with her shrugging.) "Or a boyfriend. Either way. I'm sure Mama and Daddy will be thrilled too. So stop dragging them boat-sized feet."

She was also the first person to notice my downward slide toward the end of the season . . . and to call me on it: "You got the *blues*, Jacorey Jr.," she said over breakfast one morning. "And I know something happened. You should just . . . come out."

"I should *what* now?"

"– WITH it. You should come out WITH it. Whatever's *bothering* you, I mean?"

"I don't know whatchu talking about, man."

But of course I actually did. Know. What she was talking about.

Not that she would know *this*, but even with my eyes closed right now, I can see Tremaine's kicks. Because they're seared into my memory.

And as time ticks on in what's feeling more and more like a giant coffin made of metal – that *is* kinda how train cars are shaped, is it not? – I wish I could call Jordy right now. Wish I woulda just *told* her back then.

Because she'd been right. Something had happened.

Twenty-two minutes.

I lied again. About the lack of "any real contact with Tremaine in years" thing.

I sneak another peek at the dude couple. They're now all curled up together, both with their eyes closed.

I re-shut mine.

Shit really started back in January. I'd been kinda sad. And not about anything specific either. In a very general sense. I get a little bit down every winter – not that anyone but Jordy knows that. Coaches be feelin' the same way about "that mopey-dopey shit" as they do about the whole *fear* thing. Trust.

Anyway, I had an abysmally bad game: couple travel calls, an unnecessary shot clock violation, tripped over air driving up the court and busted my lip, couldn't seem to sink a shot to save my life, had four fouls by halftime.

I was just . . . off.

So off, Coach benched me.

It had never happened before. And as dramatic as it prolly sounds, with every pity look and pat on the back and "Don't worry about it, JJ. You'll be back on next game," I felt like I was sinking lower and lower. Like tossed-overboard-with-weights-around-my-ankles type sinking.

When I got home, I went straight to my room and locked the door. Popped onto the web looking for the uhhh . . . *content* I typically turn to when I want to zone out, if you will. Stumbled onto something different than what I typically seek out. (As I think back through this sequence of events, I'm tempted to look at the dude couple again. Because . . . yeah.)

I didn't hate what I found, is the thing . . . but I also got interrupted. By my dad. Knocking on the door and saying he was checking on me. And despite him not seeing a thing, I was embarrassed to the point where I didn't pick up my tablet for a week.

Now I *do* look at the dude couple again.

What's wild about the whole thing is I'm pretty sure Jordy's right: our folks – dad included – wouldn't have a problem with me . . . liking whoever I like. Him and Ma met at a damn drag show. Her best friend from college was performing, and Dad was the bouncer at the club. I never got to meet this friend because he moved to Atlanta before I was born, but from what I understand, *he's* the one who set Ma and Dad up.

Still, though: I couldn't shake the fear of being found out. I've heard the stories where a dude like me gets caught lookin' at some shit, and suddenly the guys he's around all the time because of sports don't really wanna rock with him no more.

So my game continued to be off. Because I started having these . . . dreams. About me. And individuals like me. Me *with* individuals like me.

Guys, I mean.

Fast forward: February. By then I'd found and joined (under a different name, obviously) this site that would list different events for guys who liked guys happening around town. I'd skim through with zero intention of actually going to any of them and delete my browser history afterward, but then one popped up that was happening the day after my eighteenth birthday. A masquerade party.

I logged off.

Birthday rolled around and my teammates threw me *quite* the bash. Our center's dad owns this club uptown, and they pulled out all the stops for your boy. Fire-ass DJ, beautiful girls everywhere the eye could see. And one of them from another school, Shelley was her name, really took a liking to me. Danced me into a corner and started kissing on my neck.

And I did kiss her back – she was a great kisser, objectively speaking – and when she pushed things a bit further, I rolled with it. But we were in a club. So there was obviously a stopping point.

What's wild is . . . I was relieved about this. That there was only so far shit could go. She gave me her number and told me to call her. "You can come over and we can pick up where we left off," she said. My teammates were ecstatic, of course. "Bruh, you bagged the finest girl from Bed-Stuy Prep!"

But I knew I'd never use those digits. So I erased them.

Following night, I found myself on the train with a tux in my duffel bag.

Along with a mask.

Twenty-seven minutes on this train.

It was 10:29 p.m. when I got to the building across the street from the address attached to the masquerade listing. It had a nook where I could conceal myself in the shadows and shit.

I'd changed clothes in the bathroom at Herald Square, but was wearing a big coat so nobody could see I was in a tux underneath. The building looked sketchy as hell. Five-story brick joint on Bowery with a Chinese food spot on the ground floor. Invite said to go inside, say the password to the person behind the counter, and they'd lead me to wherever I was supposed to go.

I felt like an idiot and a half.

What if this was some kinda trap? Was I walking into a cult initiation? Was I about to get murdered? My parents – who were under the impression I'd gone to a teammate's house – had warned me about this shit, and yet here I was, standing across the street from some sketchy-ass building at the literal opposite end of the city from my warm and cozy crib in Harlem. Only God knows what horrible fate might've been awaiting me.

But then I saw a dude approaching the restaurant from my left.

He also had on a coat and was wearing a hat pulled down low over his forehead. But I woulda recognized the walk – and the kicks – just about anywhere.

Right as he reached the door, he took his hat off, and I caught a brief glimpse of Tremaine Wright's face before he slipped his mask on. Then he walked inside, and I watched through the wide front window as he raised a hand to the woman behind the counter, who dipped her head and smiled in greeting, and continued into what looked like the kind of dark hallway where the bathrooms would be.

I hurried across the street.

Just like Tremaine, I put my mask on before entering the spot. It was a full-face Black Panther joint. Wasn't taking any chances on potential recognition.

And I wound up not needing the password. "Down the hall, door at the end on the left," the woman said without looking up from whatever it was she was doing.

So I followed her directions. Was too curious at that point not to. Through the designated door and down a flight of stairs. Which led to something like nothing I'd ever seen before: guys in tuxes of assorted colors and patterns, wearing a variety of masks.

I had a bunch of "feels," as Jordy puts it, hit me at the same time. There was a little bit of fear, yeah. Still wasn't real keen on being recognized. But there was also this sense of . . . not-aloneness. Couldn't call it *belonging* per se. I was (*am*) definitely still figuring myself out. But stepping into that room – with the music thumping and dudes chit-chatting and everybody looking some form of fly – really did something for my heart, as corny as that sounds.

First funny thing of the night: only person in the spot with*out* a mask was the DJ. And I recognized him. Don't know his real name, but everybody refers to him as Twig (and he did kinda favor that one tree character from those superhero movies about the group that zips around the universe with the green lady and talking racoon).

Which I knew because he'd been the DJ at my birthday party the night before.

Definitely wouldn't be taking *my* mask off.

Though I got the impression nobody would. There were different types of masks all around the room. Some covered only the eyes, some the whole face. There was a guy in a blue paisley tux with a velvet and feathered half-face joint. A dude in black on black on black had a mask that looked like something out of *Phantom of the Opera*. Another homie in red was rocking a court jester-style piece.

Everywhere, all around, people similar to me dressed up with their faces covered.

Some were deep in conversation. Some had drinks in hand. A few looked mad pitiful checking their phones.

Basically the same stuff I saw at high school parties.

Though I guess I looked pretty pitiful, too. "First time," someone said from my right. I turned to find a dude in a teal satin-looking getup with a mask covered in peacock feathers.

So on the nose, this guy.

"Uhh . . . you could say that," I replied.

"I like your style," dude continued, giving me a once-over. "Very classic. The mask is perfect as well. Delightfully overstated. You seem like a man who knows what he wants."

Homie grinned, revealing crooked teeth.

It was time for me to go.

"'Preciate that," I said. "You have a nice night." And I turned to walk away, but dude grabbed my arm.

"Oh, don't play coy, now," he said, leaning all close and smothering my ear with his hot breath. "We're all here for the same thing –"

And just as I was about to haul off and lay dude flat on his peacocking ass, there was another voice, and a hand landed on my shoulder. "*There* you are," it said. "I been looking all over for you."

"Uhhh . . ." But before I could finish calculating how I was going to take *both* dudes out, *and* somehow manage to get away so I wouldn't get caught in at that damn party, I happened to glance down. And see a pair of white on white on white Jordan 1s.

I froze.

"My apologies," Pushy Peacock said, looking Tremaine over the same way he did me. "Didn't realize he was spoken for."

Did Tremaine know it was me? His tux was charcoal gray, by the way, and the jacket lacked lapels. Shit was maaaad clean, and his mask was a simple black one that covered the space between his eyebrows and nose. Reminded me of this sword-wielding dude who's the star of those Zorro movies my dad loves. The whole look made my stomach do a weird swoopy thing.

"All good, man," Tremaine said. "Killer 'fit, by the way. Come on, babe." And he took my hand and pulled me away.

I was too dumbstruck to do anything but go along with it.

(*Babe,* though?)

When we reached an empty tall table at the back of the room, he let go. "Super sorry about that," he said, shaking his head. "I don't usually hold people's hands without at least learning their names, but that dude is a grade-A creep, and you're *clearly* new around here. I'm Tremaine."

Confirmation.

It was weird seeing him without his camera. I was also blown that he used his true name.

My throat got tight. *How* was dude so settled about all this?

Would *I* ever get to that point?

He leaned closer. "And you are?"

"Oh . . . uhhh . . . I'm Tobias."

I waited for him to laugh or call me out. Some verification that he knew exactly who I was.

It didn't come.

"T and T!" he said, pointing to his own chest and then to me. "Nice!"

It made me laugh. And loosen up a bit . . . though not as much as I would've liked to, considering that my guilt over lying to the guy's face (mask) decided to drape its ugly self across my shoulders.

Kinda bittersweet thinking about it now.

"So tell me about yourself, *Tobias*."

Him emphasizing the name like that was a smidge suspect, but I made myself shake it off. "Whatchu wanna know?"

He shrugged. "You got any hobbies?"

"Oh, that's easy: basketball."

Regretted it instantly.

Homie didn't miss a beat, though: "Ah. A sports guy."

I laughed again. "Why you say it like that?"

"Don't get many sports guys around here." He made a visual scan of the room and I followed his eyes. "And I'm guessing you don't get a whole lotta guys like the ones in this room at your sports stuff. Is this crazy uncomfortable for you?"

"Uhhh . . ." And I decided to tell the truth. "Yeah, kinda. Between you and me, I'm not sure it would go real well if my teammates found out I came here." I didn't realize how trash

I sounded 'til the words were outta my mouth. But I couldn't figure out how to retract them. "You umm . . . come here often?" I asked, trying to change the subject.

"*Often* is a stretch. They have things like this weekly here, but this is only my third time ever coming. It's an interesting place to people watch."

"People watch?"

"Yeah. I'm super into photography and really like studying people even when I don't have my camera."

"How old are you, if you don't mind my asking?" I said then, wanting to see if he'd tell the truth.

"Turned seventeen in December." He leaned closer to me. "Don't tell anybody, but they only let me in because I know the DJ. I've photographed a lot of his sets. Technically supposed to be eighteen. And you definitely gotta watch your back for people pretending to be someone they're not."

He stared straight into my eyes when he said this, and I swear I stopped breathing.

But then he went on. "So . . . how old are you?"

"I'm . . . nineteen. College freshman. Well . . . rising sophomore now."

"You being honest about that?" And he winked.

If it had been possible to teleport out of that joint? Trust.

Guessing my silence was telling because then he said, "I'm just messing with you. Whatcha studying?"

"Umm . . . mechanical engineering. But considering changing my major."

(I *know* I sounded mad ridiculous. Why this guy continued entertaining my ass is beyond me.)

"A *smart* sports guy! Double whammy." And he busted out the smile that turns girls all goo-goo eyed and slack jawed in the halls at school. Can't even lie: with it aimed at me, the effect made perfect sense.

From there, a lot of the night is a blur. Within a couple of minutes, I'd slipped into being what I guess was some sorta dream version of a self I could eventually be: openly bisexual rising sophomore at City College with a rich on-campus life that included student government, intramural basketball, and Alpha Phi Alpha fraternity membership.

And Tremaine was crazy easy to talk to. In fact, the longer we chatted, the more stuff from my *actual* life started slipping in. I told him about feeling confused because while I knew there were *some* girls I felt attracted to, I was pretty sure I liked guys, too. (To this he said, "Same. And don't let anyone convince you your feelings are wrong. I've known I was attracted to *people* since second grade. You'd be blown away at how mad some folks get when they realize they can't box you in.")

I told him about my Jordy. ("She sounds amazing. Nothing like support from the family.")

I told him about my coaches. ("Toxic masculinity 101, my friend.")

And I told him about being nervous about not really know anything *for sure*. ("Welcome to the party. And I'm not talking about this wack one either.")

I got *so* relaxed around Tremaine Wright, when he asked if I was dating anyone, good ol' *Tobias* replied: "Well, according to what you told Peacock over there, I'm dating you."

We laughed about that, and then we kept talking.

We talked more about family: His favorite person is his older sister, Tammi, though his tour-bus driver dad, Sean, is a close second. I told him how my parents met, and he told me about his: Camille, his moms, had been a photography intern from Virginia. She'd gotten lost in the city and decided to hop on a tour bus. Soon enough, they were approaching the Flatiron Building, and her photography office was right across the street . . . so she went up to the driver and asked to be let off, but it was a nonstop tour, so he said no. She pushed harder, and when he finally looked at her, he got so distracted by her beauty, he rear-ended the cab in front of them. "Third day on the job, too," Tremaine said. "Fired instantly."

We talked about food: He's half Jamaican, but homie lives for ramen and Korean barbecue. I told him my granddad is originally from Georgia, and waxed all poetic about my love for Southern soul food.

We talked about friends: He admitted that while he knows a lot of people are "interested" in him, he's never had super close friends, especially guys. It's a thing he hopes will change once he gets to college. I told him that while I *do* have close friends – most of them my teammates – I worried about how they might react to me not being straight. "I have heard that guys' athletics can be pretty homophobic," was his response to that.

I told him he came across as real comfortable in his skin, and that I wasn't sure I'd ever get to that point. And he assured *me* that he hadn't always been that way, and that he definitely had his moments of insecurity. "Thing is, though," he said, "if I can't love and accept *myself* just as I am, why the hell would I expect anybody else to?"

A fair point, obviously.

Next thing I knew, he was checking his watch and saying he needed to leave so he wouldn't miss curfew.

And I knew I couldn't walk him out. It was too risky.

So I said it'd been nice chatting with him (who the hell did I think I *was*, yo?), and that I hoped he and I would run into each other again.

His eyes narrowed, and the corners of his mouth turned down for like the *slightest* moment, but he recovered too fast for me to mention it without seeming like I was watching him mad closely. "Yeah, man, absolutely," he said. "Guess I'll see you around."

But when homie turned to leave, I did something I still can't believe. "Yo, Tremaine," I said. And I reached for his arm. When he turned back to me, I lifted the bottom of my mask, closed the space between us . . . and I kissed him right on the mouth.

"Okay, then," is all he said when we broke apart (after . . . some time).

What felt like eighty-three minutes, but was likely only a few awkward seconds, passed. "You should uhh . . . prolly get going, huh?" I said to break the intense silence. And also probably because I was feeling too many things at once: shock over my boldness; guilt over not asking permission to kiss him (that's something I *can* say about my parents: they real serious about the *consent* thing); sadness that we were about to part ways; excitement from the lip-locking; fear about what that excitement was confirming for me. The way I felt kissing Tremaine was *far* different than I'd felt with ol' girl Shelley the night before.

Shit was terrifying.

"Yeah . . ." he said. "I guess maybe I should—"

There's a loud *thump* and a collective gasp on the train, and my eyes fly open.

"Oh my God, is he okay?"

The words register before the lump on the ground does, but when my brain finally connects the dots between Tremaine's empty seat and the white-on-white-on-white kicks attached to the body on the grimy-ass train floor, I'm up and then down beside him before I even realize what I'm doing.

"Yo, Tremaine!" I shake his shoulder. Panic starts to make my palms damp and my pits sweaty . . . just like it did in sixth grade.

You'd think I woulda learned something about being helpful when I see a guy in distress since then, right? Just shameful.

"Tremaine!" Another shake. "Man, you all right?"

Dumb-ass question.

But he groans.

Good sign in my book.

"Tremaine, it's me, JJ," I say, moving to shift him to his back. "Imma get you outta here, man, but if you could help me a lil bit by letting me know you can hear me, I'd really appreciate it."

Groans again.

I stretch his legs out and then move back up to his head. Start fanning his face like I seen folks do in movies.

Zero clue what I'm *actually* doing, by the way.

But it seems to be working. His head slowly moves to the right, then to the left. And once it's back to center, his eyes open.

I think my heart does a tap dance or somethin'.

"Thank God," I say. Legit crossing myself. "Yo, can you move at all? I wanna get you up and off this train, but if I gotta carry you, Imma need to strategize—"

"JJ?" he says, all groggy and confused. (And damn do I have a love/hate relationship with what it does to me inside. Gotta avoid looking at his mouth.)

"Yeah, man. It's me."

"What happened? Where are we?" His eyes drift shut again.

"Nah, bruh. You gotta stay awake. We're on the subway. There was a blackout and we been stuck in a tunnel for like thirty minutes."

"I hate enclosed spaces," he says.

"That's what I know. But what I *need* to know is if you think you can walk. Imma get the door open, and then I'll help you up and you can let me know, cool?"

"Mmhmm," he says. Well, *hums*.

Quick as a flash I've got my keys out of my pocket and am using the tiny knife on my foldable mini-multitool keychain thing to pop open the panel above the car's center doors (thank God I'm tall enough to easily reach it). I'm sure most people don't even notice it when getting on and off the train, but when I was little, my dad made me learn how to get myself off of *all* public transportation in case of an emergency.

He's also the person who makes me carry the tool.

Once I'm inside the compartment, I flip the two red levers – the *click* of the doors unlocking almost sounds like music – and throw all my weight into pushing the doors open.

Then it's back to Tremaine.

"Okay, Imma lift you by the shoulders to sit you up, then I'll slip my arms under yours and wrap 'em around your waist to pull you to your feet, cool?"

I don't wait for a response this time.

Once I've got him up – side note: dude is *heavy* – and I'm holding him around the waist while he gets his feet beneath him, I ask him again: "You think you can walk?"

His head drops back against my shoulder. (Startles the hell outta me.) "Yeah. With assistance."

"I gotchu," I say. "Pretty sure we gone have to walk single file to get out this tunnel, but you can lean against my back."

I shift to his right without letting go of him completely, and pull his arm over my shoulder before stepping in front of him. Someone comes over and hands me *both* of our backpacks, and by some wiggly magic, I'm able to get them both on my front

– thank God *they're* not heavy. And then his weight settles onto me, and we make our way to the open doors.

Within seconds, we're off. I know some people follow, but I stay focused on getting *us* to open air.

Full disclosure: subway tunnels *outside* the train? Real scary shit. Definitely regret my middle school horror film phase. Little rinky-dink cell phone flashlight is only marginally helpful.

We walk, maaaaaad slow, for what feels like an eternity, his whole front pressed against my whole back (which is *a lot*). I'm holding his right arm against my chest with my left hand so I can hold the light with my right. Train was just shy of the 96th Street station.

So I do my best to focus on dude's weight against me and the knowledge that it's on me to get *him* out of this damn hole in the ground, and by some strange-ass magic, it keeps my feet moving.

Soon, the space is opening up, and I couldn't be more relieved.

"I can walk easier now, I think," Tremaine says once we're almost at the station. His weight lessens a bit, then he pulls his arm off me completely.

"You sure?"

"Yeah. I could also be helpful. Let me get that bag."

"Nah, man, chill out. I got it."

"So JJ Harding's a gentleman, huh?" And I can't see the look on his face, but I'm glad 'cause it means he can't see mine either.

Truth be told, I wasn't paying attention to which direction we were headed, but the moment we're on the platform, which honestly feels even darker than the train did, it's like all the energy drains outta me. "Yo, you mind if we cool it here for a minute?"

Before he can even answer, I'm feeling my way to the wall and sliding down like the condensation on the side of a cup. Probably not the cleanest floor to be sitting on – especially in my new jeans – but I couldn't get back up right now if I tried.

I feel a body settle in beside me. Like reaaaaal close.

"You all right, man?" Tremaine's voice is low, but thick in the dark. I can hear other people making their way onto the platform – lots of talk about finding an exit – but Tremaine's bare arm against mine makes me feel like it's okay to just . . . sit.

"I'll admit: I've been better."

He laughs. And though fifteen minutes ago, I wouldn't have been ready to acknowledge how it makes me feel, right now? With him this close – and safe?

Shit's incredible. Real glad it's dark because I would probably be tryna sneak peeks at his mouth.

"Definitely feel you on *that* one," he says. "When that train stopped . . . well, let's just say I knew things were headed downhill fast. Whole enclosed space thing is a no-go for me. Being on the train doesn't bother me so much as long as we're in motion. But being stopped? In a *tunnel*? The claustrophobia got *very* real."

"Like in sixth grade?" I ask.

"Yeah, pretty much."

"I uhhh . . ." Am I really about to say this? "I could tell you were struggling a little bit. I'm sorry I didn't act sooner."

"I mean, with *your* track record . . ." And he bumps my shoulder with his. My stomach feels like it just went up for a 360-degree dunk in my throat.

Which I clear. "Are you okay, though?" I ask.

"Oh, you know . . . just literally fainted on a subway car full of strangers."

"Guess it's a good thing none of them could actually see you."

He laughs again.

It's too much, man.

"You know, I gotta tell you," he says, "Despite your heroics – hesitant though they may have been – you look a lot better without the Black Panther mask."

I can't even breathe, let alone speak.

"I saw you at Herald Square that night. You were coming out the bathroom in your tux – very fresh by the way – and I followed you at a distance. Got on the F on the same car as you, just at the other end. I thought – hoped, really – you might be headed to the same place I was, but it didn't seem possible. Jump-Jump Harding at a masquerade party for queer guys?"

Won't lie: despite everything he's telling me, I smile at the sound of him saying my nickname. Also didn't miss that *hoped* he said.

"When you got off at Second Avenue, I was floored. I didn't split off from you until you tucked yourself into that building across the street from where the party was happening. And after waiting a few minutes to see what you would do, I went on in, really hoping you would follow me."

"And I did."

"Yup."

I take a deep breath now. Honestly sorta relieved . . . but also annoyed if you want the truth. "So you knew exactly who I was the whole time."

"Sure did. And Imma be honest with you, JJ," he says, "I was pretty mad at you. I gave you my *real* name hoping it would encourage you to give me yours. But you didn't."

Welp. There goes *my* annoyance.

"For weeks – WEEKS, JJ! – I was conflicted. I've had a crush on you since even *before* the whole sixth grade locker room thing. I loved talking to you and learning more about your life. You didn't realize it, but you actually mentioned your sister by name at one point."

"Well, damn."

"Right. You were *you* . . . but pretending you weren't. And I didn't know what to do with that. Especially since you knew I was me. And that kiss—"

"That kiss." The words are out in the air before I can catch them.

"Yeah," he says. "Don't get me wrong: I enjoyed it. Which I'm sure you could tell: I didn't exactly push you away."

I'm glad it's dark cuz that makes me cheese like a damn kindergartner who got an A+ on a crayon project.

"But I also kinda hated myself for getting *any* pleasure out of it, JJ. You were lying to me the whole time *and* you kissed me without my permission. It was confusing."

"I'm sorry, Tremaine," I say. "Like real, real, *real* sorry, man."

He doesn't say anything, and I don't say anything else, so we just sit there. I check my phone and am surprised to see that using the flashlight for forty minutes hasn't affected my battery life too much.

I wonder if this is some kinda metaphor.

"Yo, why didn't you say anything?" I ask Tremaine then.

"You know, I'm not sure," he says. "I've been asking myself that for weeks. Why didn't I just call you out? I still don't really have an answer. I guess like . . . well, I get needing some space and time to figure yourself out. Though I will say: based on what you told me about your parents, I do think your sis is right about them likely being supportive."

I nod. "You know, that's something I figured out while we were walking up outta that tunnel, T. It's not that I think my parents will take issue with me liking who I like. It's more the basketball thing. There's only ever been one openly gay NBA player."

"Jason Collins," he says.

I'm impressed. "Right. And yeah, he got a lot of support or whatever. But it's been like a few years, and nobody else has come out. In sports there's just this . . ." And I pause, not really knowing what word to use.

"Stigma," he says.

So I guess I can check off "finishes my sentences" on the Ideal Partner list.

"Right. And while my folks won't take issue with my . . . orientation, I suppose is the right word, they not gone be too keen on me not hoopin'. In their minds – and in mine too until recently – that's my ticket to college tuition. And even though I'm not sure I even *want* to hoop anymore, being *out* will potentially mean being *on the outs* with my teammates and coaches, which would obviously mess up my whole game. I'm sure they'll all *act* supportive – nobody wants to be labeled a homophobic. But this shit runs deep, man."

I hear him sigh beside me.

We're quiet for a few minutes as my dilemma settles in the dark around us. I have no idea what I'm gonna do.

I will say, though: some of the pressure on my chest has loosened. Knowing *someone* else knows my secret and isn't looking at me all different is . . . helpful.

Baby steps, I guess.

"You were headed to that party Kareem is DJing at in Brooklyn?" I say just to be saying something.

"Yeah. Gotta take pictures."

"That's what I figured. I was too."

"No surprise there." I can hear the smile in his voice.

"So uhhh . . . how we gonna get there now?"

He looks up at the station sign. "I mean, we *are* near the park . . ." He turns to me. "Bike it? I'm sure we could grab a couple of rentals. Yeah, we'll be sweaty as hell when we get there but . . . at least we'll get there. You down?"

"Hell yeah, I'm down," I say. "Actually sounds kinda fun."

"Hey, JJ?"

It's crazy how much I dig the sound of those two letters coming out of his mouth. "Yeah, Tremaine?"

"Can we agree that you won't ever lie to me like that again?"

Shit hits hard. "Yeah, man. Again: I'm sorry."

"I forgive you. This time."

I laugh. Feels real good. "I can respect that."

"If you want the truth – and you better not use it against me: I don't think I could *really* stay mad at you."

"You know, I think I've had a thing for you, too, since that day in sixth grade," I finally admit. "Though I obviously tried to deny it."

Now he laughs. "Good to hear, man."

We lapse back into quiet, but the dark is starting to make me itch.

"You think the lights will come back on soon?" I ask.

He doesn't respond immediately, but I don't press. Just . . . sit. No idea what comes next or where we go from here.

But I also find that I don't really care. Not in this moment.

Just when I think he's not gonna answer, he does: "I don't know. But I hope so."

It occurs to me: "Is the darkness messing with your claustrophobia? Anything I can do to help?"

He laughs again. "Nah, that's not it at all," he says, leaning into me. I swear if *melting* was a literal thing, I'd be a puddle of goop on this floor instead of a person.

He goes on: "I'm honestly not scared at all right now. Just looking forward to seeing you with your mask off."

THE LONG WALK
ACT 2

Tiffany D. Jackson

Central Park, 6:05 p.m.

Kareem and I head down Broadway, the humidity making it hard to breathe, and it feels like we're trekking across the surface of the sun. Or maybe it's because Kareem is walking like a damn speed racer and I'm jogging to keep up. By the time we reach the top of Central Park, I'm covered in sweat.

"Damn," I gasp. "Why you walking so fast?"

He sucks his teeth. "Why you walking so slow? Some of us got places to be!"

"Hmph. Damn, she really got you whipped, huh?"

"What was that?" He spins around and I run right into his chest with a thud. He has . . . muscles? When did he get those? His arms are filled out. And he even has some facial hair.

I pat down my edges nervously, and maneuver past him. "Nothing."

He hangs back, as if debating whether he should go through with this crazy plan of his. I've been debating the same thing for the last thirty minutes.

I can't be stuck in the city with no money, and he definitely ain't leaving me and my phone, his only contact to the world. We're all we got right now, whether we like it or not.

He catches up to me, slowing his pace by a fraction, and we walk in silence for a few minutes, down Central Park West, bordering the biggest park in NYC. Plopped right in the middle of Manhattan, it has meadows, woods, fountains, lakes, gardens, playgrounds, restaurants, a zoo, and even a castle. It's also full of bougie rich people and their ankle-biting dogs (I like Prospect Park in Brooklyn better).

Daddy always laughs while telling us stories of tourists being lost for hours in the middle of the day because they can't find an exit. I hope they find their way out of there before the sun goes down.

"Not that it's any of your business," Kareem starts. "But I'm supposed to deejay at Twig's block party tonight."

Block party? I didn't know about that. Guess that's another thing that happens when you stop being someone's girlfriend: you stop getting invited to stuff like your neighbor's annual blow-out block party. Almost everyone goes.

"How they gonna have a party with no power?" I ask.

"Said he's gonna get a backup generator."

I shake my head. "That don't make sense."

"Don't gotta make sense. Twig's paying me eight hundred for this party and I need the money. But he ain't gonna pay me shit if I'm not there and ready to go."

I shrug. "Well, with all these parties you got lined up, maybe you don't really need that internship."

He chuckles. "Nice try. But every dollar counts. You ain't the only one trying to go to school in the fall."

My heart cracks but he probably can't hear it over the traffic jam, so I keep my face straight. We were supposed to go to college together. That was always our plan. Now he has new plans. Plans I know nothing about. Kind of wish I hadn't unfollowed him on social media. Then I'd know what school he's going to. It's not like I want to ask because then he'll think I care, and I definitely don't.

"Oh," I mutter, struggling to hide the hurt in my voice. "Well, guess we'll see which one of us she picks."

"What'd you need that job for anyways? Ain't your daddy paying for school?"

There's a bitterness in his question but I ignore it.

"Yeah."

"But?"

The idea of telling him swishes around my head until I relent.

"Well . . . there's this special program that'll let me start school early and earn credits."

"Early? Like, leave for school early?"

"August eighth," I say proudly. "And I'm trying to pay for it myself!"

He looks away, palming his knuckles. "Oh. So . . . you'll be gone for our birthdays?"

"Oh. Uh . . . yeah. I guess so."

Kareem's birthday is August fourteenth. Mine is the thirteenth. He used to joke that he loved the idea of being with an older woman for a whole twenty-four hours. We haven't spent a birthday apart in seven years, and it wasn't until he brought it up that I felt the pinch of this lost tradition. Recognizing that nothing will ever be the same, between us or with life in general.

Still (and yeah, I know I shouldn't be thinking this), it feels real good walking with him, side by side, just the two of us again. We used to take long walks all the time. Well, not this long, maybe around a few blocks or so. This is on some other level. But before, those warm summer nights always made us bubbly, like we were falling in love for the first time. We'd lazily drift down the streets, shoulders bumping into each other, as if we'd forgotten how to walk straight, only stopping so he could retie my sneakers like he used to when we were kids. Nothing but cheesy grins, hand-holding, and kissing.

Lots of kissing.

Scenes right out of those old Black romance movies from the '90s my mom put me on to. The same kind I want to write and direct someday. Well, maybe. Not sure if I believe in happy endings anymore. Probably end up doing those depressing art house films instead.

"Heard you going to Clark Atlanta," he says, flatly. "Congrats . . . I guess."

I shake the memory away, crossing my arms.

"You guess? You knew I wanted to go to college." We were

supposed to go together, I almost add but stop myself.

"I know! You had that whole list, but I thought NYU was your first choice. Film school."

Just hearing "NYU" makes my throat clench. "Yeah . . . well, Clark Atlanta has a media program too."

"Hm. Guess I never thought you'd really want to go so far from home . . . so soon." He shrugs. "Guess things change."

"Don't you mean you've changed?" I snap.

As we reach the corner of Eighty-Sixth Street, he ignores that last dig and quickly stretches out his arm. My heart balloons. He still doesn't like me crossing without holding his hand, even with standstill traffic. Always so protective . . .

"Aye, lemme see the phone real quick," he says, wiggling his fingers.

Pop! Heart deflates.

"Why?"

"What you mean 'why?' I need to make a call, that's why!"

"Who you got to call?"

"Yo, why you trying to be all up in my business?"

He's already called Twig and his mom. Who else is left except–

"Ugh!" I shout. "Are you for real right now?"

"What?"

"You're trying to call HER? On MY phone!"

He sucks his teeth. "Come on now, I'm not stupid."

"Then who you calling?"

"Yo, quit playing. I told you, we gotta work together, then –"

"Then what? You can go back to ignoring me? That's what you want, right?"

I dig the phone out of my purse and slap it into his hand. "Here. Call whoever!"

He stares at the phone for a minute, gripping it tight, about to turn it into dust.

"You know, it's funny how you got so much to say to me now when you been the one ignoring me!"

"What? You're the one acting brand-new –"

"Yo, why you being mad difficult right now? Don't you want to get back home to your real bae, the TV?"

Low. Blow.

"Don't try to act like she ain't got you so whipped that you trying to stomp across the entire city to get back to her!"

"Man, whatever! You the one who broke up with *me*. Remember?"

That's . . . not exactly true. Yeah, I sent him a text. But I didn't exactly break up with him. I didn't say the words "we're done." What I said made everything a hazy gray. So really, it was his silence that finished us off. At least that's what I tell myself.

"What? Got nothing to say now," he snarls before turning his back to me, stepping closer to the street, letting the traffic drown out his voice. Because he doesn't want me to know who he's talking to, when before, we told each other everything. Guess that doesn't matter anymore.

A girl in overalls exits the underpass from the park with a giant black pit bull. We back out of their way and she gives Kareem a curious once-over, walking by.

Wait . . . is she really checking him out? Right in front of me! Like I'm not standing right here? Well, six feet away from him.

Everyone told me to be careful with Kareem. "Girl, it's gonna be hard keeping him!" my cousins had told me when we first started dating. "Tall, perfect teeth, a cute-ass smile. He's a pretty boy. You can't trust those types."

Yeah, I guess he's cute, but he's also Kareem, the one who can burp the alphabet, rarely uses utensils properly, and thinks Teenage Mutant Ninja Turtles 2 deserved an Oscar. Didn't think I had much to worry about.

Until I saw it for myself. How all the girls slyly made it known they wanted him. Random text messages, hearts under every online photo, music requests in class. He didn't seem to notice the thirst, but I did. I just never imagined he'd prove everyone right.

"You were probably going to break up after high school anyways," my sister had said after it happened. "I mean, you're pretty and all but he probably wanna be with chicks who be out in these streets. You don't even like going to the supermarket when it's crowded. And if you think high school girls are bad, college girls are a whole different beast. Just be glad it happened now."

And I am glad . . . for the most part. I moved on, took a different route to school, sold my prom ticket, accepted Clark Atlanta, and made Kareem a forbidden subject in the house.

As far as I was concerned, he ceased to exist. I don't even think about him . . . well, that much . . . anymore. But seeing him today totally blindsided me. All I know is, I need that job so I can get out of this city.

Then, I'll never have to see Kareem again.

MADE TO FIT

Ashley Woodfolk

A brownstone, 6:37 p.m.
I'm stomping out a literal fire when she walks in with her dog.
And all the senior citizens are screaming.

"Nella, be careful!"

"Don't distract her!"

"This is your fault in the first place!"

"Yeah, Mordy!"

"Oh, shut up, Aida, wouldja?"

"Do you want us to be homeless?"

"Or worse – dead!"

"Won't be long now for you anyway."

"Can everyone just shut up?"

Seconds later, I'm breathing hard and standing over a singed playing card, which is still partially under my boot. The elderly residents of Althea House, one member of the senior living facility's staff, and the girl in the doorway are staring at me. I'm looking down at the carpet. There's a hole burned into the bluish-greenish rug and I can see clear through it to the hardwood underneath, even though the rec room is lit only by a dozen or so candles.

"Whoa," the girl in the doorway whispers. She's surrounded by a halo of light because the sun hasn't set yet. The room we're in is pretty dim, but it's still light enough to see her. And she's gorgeous.

She's wearing overalls with a white midriff tank underneath, and I feel peak-gay when my eyes immediately go to the strip of soft-looking brown skin I can see beneath the denim. She has a ton of thick, dark hair, and it's twisted into two heavy braids, one flopped over each of her narrow shoulders. She has a handful of silver bangles on each wrist and they tinkle every time her dog moves because she's holding the leash so loosely.

Her dog – an all-black pit bull with a wrinkly muzzle – has a blue bandanna tied around his neck and is wearing a vest that says Love on a Leash. His wags his tail so hard it looks like he's twerking.

The girl's wire-rimmed glasses are a little crooked and they're sliding down her wide nose. But she pushes them back up, smiles at me, and slow claps.

I'm not proud to admit it, but staring is one of my (many) vices. And I'm still straight-up ogling her when my phone starts buzzing against my thigh. I jump like I've been caught cheating, knowing it's a text from Bree, and my heart is racing, but I can't tell if it's because of my recent stint as a literal fire extinguisher, the message waiting for me, or the girl in the doorway.

I check my phone. It is a message from Bree. I swallow hard and don't write back.

"Okay!" Mimi, the director of enrichment, says. She was leading the activities and was the one who suggested playing cards in a room full of candles. I suggested not playing in the windowless rec room during a blackout, but she disagreed. Said it would provide "atmosphere." I glare at her as she claps her hands once, loud. "Card game over."

"No shit, Sherlock," says Queenie, my favorite old broad in this joint, tossing the rest of her cards on the table.

"I'm no good at poker anyway," Miss Sadie says, shrugging. She used to be a kindergarten teacher and it shows. Everything from her pink cardi to her soft voice makes me want to recite nursery rhymes.

Pearl, who pretends to be above it all, elbows her best friend, Birdie, who just moved in. "Told you these people were crazy," Pearl says, and Birdie looks nervous and adds, "Yeah, but at least it's distracting me from thinking about how dark it's gonna be in here in a few hours."

Aida shakes her head, adjusts her hijab, and rolls her eyes at her husband, Mordechai, whose yarmulke is crooked atop his balding head, while setting down her cards too. (I still don't know how the two of them ended up together.)

Grandpop Ike sighs and puts his heavy hand on my shoulder. "Good job, kiddo," he says, looking down at the burned rug. But I'm still looking at her.

"Thank God you're here, Joss," I hear Mimi say as she walks

over to the girl in the doorway. "I know it's going to be a long night, and Mordechai already almost burned the place down. If Nella hadn't been here . . ."

So this is Joss. Which means this dog is the all-time famous –

"Ziggy!" Mordechai shouts. He's rolling his wheelchair across the room, leaning over to scratch the dog behind the ears as Joss says, "Oh, you remember Ziggy today, huh? What about me? Who am I, Mr. M?"

"You're Jocelyn Williams, of course," Mordechai says without hesitation, and I grin, pleasantly surprised. It's touch and go when it comes to his memory these days. "What is it you kids say?" he continues. "Duh?"

Joss is laughing and now she's hugging Mimi and telling her she came as quickly as she could. It's like all the residents of Althea House have forgotten about the mortal danger they were in seconds ago because Joss and Ziggy are here now and nothing else matters. Ziggy is still doing his butt-shaking tail wag and is licking Mordechai's face, and I've never seen Mr. M so happy. Even Aida, who is normally a total grump, is smiling, and when Ziggy flips onto his back, she bends down and gives him a belly rub.

Joss walks over to me and extends one of her jangly arms. I look at her bracelets and then up at her eyes. They're such a dark shade of brown that they look black, and her gaze feels as heavy as the color. "Hey. You must be Ike's granddaughter. He talks about you all the time. I'm Joss, and don't tell anyone but," she steps closer and whispers, "your grandpa is my favorite."

Pop totally hears her, and he wiggles his eyebrows. "Feeling's mutual, little lady," he says.

I'm remembering all the things Grandpop Ike has said about Jocelyn, the girl who brings her therapy-certified dog to Althea House every Tuesday afternoon. That she's pretty and sweet and so, so smart. That her dog has the purest soul on earth. That together they seem almost too good to be true. That I'd love her if we ever met. "I think Joss likes the ladies too, boo," he told me with a wink just last week; icing on the She's-Perfect-for-You cake he's been baking since school let out for the summer, and really since I came out to him. I've never had a girlfriend, and it seems like everyone is really invested in changing that for me before I go to college.

It's why I've avoided visiting him on Tuesdays – I didn't want to bump into Joss and Ziggy, the dynamic duo he was convinced I'd be obsessed with.

But now, even though it's a Friday, they're here. And I'm here. I can't hide from the possibility of her anymore, even in the steadily growing dark.

I swallow hard and reach for her hand, reminding myself that I can't afford to fall for another perfect girl. When people seem too good to be true, they usually are, and if I learned anything at all from Bree, it's that.

"Hey," I say, trying to push thoughts of Bree far, far away. "Cute dog."

"I know, right?" Joss says, glancing back at him. "Zig's the best." She looks at the burned carpet and makes a face. "So, like, what exactly happened?"

Althea House is an actual house: a hundred-year-old, ivy-covered brownstone on the Upper West Side where a pair of best friends, Marie-Jeanne Beauvais and Althea Walker, had lived together after their children grew up and their husbands passed away. They were friends until the literal end, and when Althea died suddenly a decade ago, Marie-Jeanne converted their house into a senior living facility and named it after her friend, hoping it would bring joy to the later years of other senior citizens' lives the way it had for them.

Everyone calls Marie-Jeanne the Madame of Althea House, and though we often see her granddaughter, Lana, coming and going, we rarely see Marie-Jeanne herself.

The brownstone's two top floors are home to the twelve residents – split between seven rooms (four doubles, three singles) and the attic apartment where Marie-Jeanne lives – and the main floor has a spacious living and dining area, the rec room, and a big, bright kitchen. The basement is at once the staff's office, laundry room, and nurses' station. Althea House has been my refuge all summer, the only place I've gone other than work and home. Grandpop Ike likes it here, too, and he hasn't liked much of anything since Granny Zora died in January, so that's really saying something.

I flop onto the big L-shaped couch and inspect the sole of my boots. The rubber doesn't seem to be melted and that feels like some kind of small miracle.

"After the lights went out and everyone started to panic, Mimi thought it would be a good idea to try to maintain some of the activities she'd already planned for the evening. You know, to keep everyone occupied and hopefully calm – so we could all ride out the blackout in peace. So poker is what happened," I say, answering Joss's question. "The game was getting a little heated," I continue, and Pop cackles. I roll my eyes and sock Pop in the arm. "No pun intended. But Mr. M got upset when he had to fold for the third time in a row."

"He threw his cards," Pearl says, and Birdie nods.

"Like a child throwing a tantrum," Queenie says from the other end of the couch while examining her manicured nails.

"We could have died," Mr. Alec Montgomery-Allen adds dramatically, clutching his knitting needles, a bundle of pale yarn, and what looks like the beginning of a blanket. His husband, Todd (the other Mr. Montgomery-Allen), nods and pulls his sweater (knit by Alec) around his shoulders more tightly, even though, since the air conditioner went out with the rest of the power, it's getting warmer in here by the second. I hope the humidity doesn't shrink my fro.

"One of the cards skimmed a candle, caught fire, fell onto the carpet," I say, picking up the story again. "Then Mr. M blew on it. Like, I think he thought he could blow it out like you'd blow out a candle or something."

"Except the floor isn't a goddamn birthday cake," Queenie says, fluffing her silver afro. Her hair is almost as big as mine.

I snort.

"Right," Mr. Todd Montgomery-Allen agrees. "It most certainly is not."

"I woulda done the same thing, honey," Birdie whispers to Mordechai and pats his leg.

"So the *itty-bitty* fire got a tiny bit bigger," Pop says, like we're all being ridiculous. And maybe we kind of are, but it was fire. "That's when Nella-Bear sprang into action." He squeezes my shoulder again like he's proud.

Sadie chimes in and whispers, "Mimi was texting, so she didn't even notice until I screamed. Can you believe it?"

Joss presses her lips together, I think to keep from laughing, but then she shakes her head seriously. She can totally believe it, her eyes say. Mimi loves the residents, but the woman texts more than I text with Bree. (Which is to say, a lot.)

"So anyway," I continue, "I stomped on it. By then everyone was screaming, not just Miss Sadie. That's when you walked in."

"Wow," Joss says, her dark eyes on me again. "Sounds like you saved the day."

I don't think I've done anything exceptional. I'm too used to being the one who gets saved, not the one who does the saving. But when she looks at me the way she's looking at me right now, like I'm some kind of hero, I can't help but feel a little heroic.

Pretty quickly after that, everyone moves into the living room where we, thankfully, don't need to use any candles yet. The Montgomery-Allens go back to knitting, Queenie pulls out her reading glasses and a smutty-looking romance novel, Miss Sadie starts chatting with Mimi, and everyone else, including Aida and Mordechai, surround Ziggy.

Joss reaches into the pink fanny pack she's wearing and hands a baggie full of dog treats to Grandpop Ike. Then without saying another word to anyone, she strides purposefully over to the grand piano near the bay window, where the sun is blessing the living room with enough light to see the individual curls that fuzz around Joss's temples. I try hard not to stare. And when she starts playing something contemporary and upbeat, I can't help but think, Who the hell is this girl?

Grandpop Ike doesn't head over to Ziggy with the treats, even though the dog has spotted them and his tail is thump, thump, thumping against the floor in anticipation. Pop's watching me watch her.

I cross my arms and pull my eyes away. "What?" I ask through clenched teeth.

"Toldja you'd like her," he says, then he drops this bomb before heading in Ziggy's direction: "She sings too."

And I don't know how I'm going to survive an entire evening with a girl like Jocelyn Williams.

My phone buzzes again. Another text from Bree. Like she can feel my spark of interest in someone other than her.

I heard there's a blackout in the city.

You good?

My ex-friend-with-imagined-benefits, (What do you even call someone you used to dream about kissing but never came close to actually kissing?) is spending the summer in Haiti, working at a children's hospital that regularly loses electricity, and she's checking on me. If I'm heroic, she's basically Wonder Woman. Which is ironic, because she looks a bit like an Afro-Latinx Gal Gadot (darker skin and curlier hair, but just as gorgeous).

I'm good, I send back quickly. I have to force my thumb not to scroll up, so I won't get lost in the things we used to say to each other. (Obsessively rereading texts is another vice of mine.)

I have another message too: this one from my cousin, Twig.

TWIG: **Hey cuz, what time you gettin back to BK?**

NELLA: **Well hello to you too Twiggy-boo.**

TWIG: **Yo, you betta not call me that in public.**

NELLA: **Lol. I dunno. 9ish? With this blackout tho, I might not even make it.**

TWIG: **You HAVE to cuzzo! The block party's gonna be poppin. Nothing else to do tonight with the lights out anyway. Do me a solid and pick up more cups?**

I tuck my phone away and shove my hands into my pockets. My cousin Twig is another person who is very invested in my love life, and he is always making me go to parties. He actually introduced me to Bree ("I think this chick I know likes chicks too, cuz!") by dragging me to a house party I wanted to skip. So I didn't have the heart to break it to him when what happened between me and Bree happened. Or rather, didn't happen. He and everyone else on our block will be expecting me to show up at the party with her because we've been inseparable for months. They don't know the truth about us, or more importantly about her. Just like I didn't. I slide my hands down my face and groan, but no one notices.

"I met my Zora during one of these things," I hear Pop say, just as Joss's fingers go still on the piano. The Costas, who weren't on the main floor with the rest of us, walk down the long front staircase. Joss turns, sees them, and smiles.

"Maria! Santiago! Glad you could join us," she says cheerfully.

"Well, when we heard the piano, we thought it might be you down here," Maria says, and I feel my jaw drop. I've only seen the Costas once all summer because they're normally holed up together in their room watching telenovelas and making out like teenagers. And I've never seen Marie-Jeanne. I'm not even sure she's real.

"During one of what things?" Joss asks, turning to Pop. She's somehow listening to everyone at once.

"He's talking about the 1977 blackout," I tell her.

"That's right, Nella-Bear. That's right; 1977 it was. I'll never forget it."

Pop gets this faraway look in his eyes, the same one he gets whenever he talks about Granny. My chest feels tight because I miss her more when he brings her up, but it makes him so happy that I'd never ask him not to.

Joss says, "Well, don't stop talking now. I need to hear the rest of this story." She closes the piano and props her elbows on the lid. Her thick braids fall behind her lifted shoulders.

Pop grins.

"I noticed her right away. The day she moved in. It was her

smile. She had the deepest dimples I'd ever seen on a woman. But she ain't even know I existed," he starts, and everyone, even Ziggy, seems to be listening. The dog curls up right by Pop's feet and lays his big head on the toe of Aida's orthopedic sneaker. Queenie folds her book closed and Alec and Todd stop knitting. Pearl and Birdie smirk. Mimi even puts down her phone.

"I was the super in her building. And I was trying to tell the tenants to stay inside because everyone was going nuts, looting, setting fires. The whole city was a mess. But she was dead-set on walking all the way across town to check on her mama."

I smile. I've heard this story dozens of times before, but I still love it, even more so since we lost Granny Z a few months ago. I turn around and kneel on the couch so I can look at him while he tells this part. It was just like my grandmother to go to any length for a person she loved.

"That girl. Head hard as a rock, even then. She wouldn't listen. Trains wasn't running, buses neither, and it was a half-hour walk, easy, without them. We argued for damn near forty-five minutes about it. But because I'd had a crush on her for months, I finally relented. Told her if she had to go, I was going with her. And she smiled so big and wide when I agreed, those puddle-deep dimples taking over her whole face, that I knew no matter what happened I'd made the right choice."

"Okay, so, I definitely need to hear the rest of this," Joss interrupts. "But do you have a picture of her?" She looks around and says, "I can't be the only one who wants to see those dimples!"

"Oh, we know what she looks like," Todd says. And everyone in the room nods.

Grandpop Ike shows his favorite photo of Granny to people constantly. Everyone here has definitely seen it, and I'm actually really surprised Joss hasn't. Sadie even painted a portrait of Granny Zora based on the photo and gave it to Pop for his birthday. It's hanging on the wall in his room.

Grandpop Ike smiles. He reaches into his pocket and pulls out his wallet. But when he pushes back the thin flap that's usually just in front of the well-worn photograph of my Granny Zora, he makes a strange face.

"Hm," Pop says. He turns his back to us, empties his wallet, and then the rest of his pockets before turning around. Folded receipts, credit cards, a few wrinkled bills, and a dozen coins clatter onto the little side table closest to him.

"You good?" Queenie asks. But Pop looks at the table, then turns in a circle. "Hm," he says again.

He walks over to the coat rack by the door and turns the pockets of his jacket inside out. They're empty already, and now Pop is starting to look stressed.

"Uh, Mimi? You seen the photo of my Zora anywhere?"

Mimi shakes her head. "I don't think so," she says.

Pop walks to the couch and lifts the cushions, even tells me and Queenie to stand up so he can look under the ones we'd been sitting on.

"I don't know where it could be," he says. "Nella, you know how much I love that picture."

I nod, thinking of the day we got Granny's diagnosis. The day when he tucked the photo into his wallet and everything started to change.

"Pop," I say. "Don't worry. It's gotta be here somewhere. You haven't even left Althea House in like three days, right?"

He nods, but his eyes are still darting around the room like the photo is right in front of him, he just isn't seeing it.

"So we'll look for it when the lights come back on," I promise him. "We'll find it."

But he shakes his head. "No, kiddo, you don't understand. That photo hasn't left my sight since the day I moved out of our apartment. I need it back now."

Pop is level-headed when it comes to just about everything. Except Granny Zora. He went to a really dark place after she passed. It was why Mom thought it would be a good idea for him to move in here instead of staying in the apartment he'd lived in with Granny for forty years. It was a fight to get him out of their two-bedroom Harlem walk-up, but here Pop has built-in friends, no bills to pay, and me and Mom don't have to worry that he's not eating or that he's spending all day sitting around alone.

Pop heads for the stairs and trips on the first one, probably because the hallway is more shadowed than normal.

"Pop!" I jog over and grab his arm. I pull him up even though he caught himself with one hand and didn't fall all the way down. "I'll look for it now, okay? You just go chill in the living room. I don't want you to, like, break a hip, old man."

He kinda smiles, but it doesn't reach his eyes. Maybe because this blackout is reminding him so much of the summer he met Granny.

I walk him back over to the couch in the living room. Sadie puts a hand on his shoulder and Aida hands him Ziggy's treats from where he'd dropped them when he first reached into his wallet for the picture.

"Ziggy," Joss says from the piano. She'd jumped up when Grandpop Ike tripped. She walks over to where Pop has sat down and points to him. "Lap," she says. And Ziggy pads over and puts both his paws on Pop's lap. He rests his head on top and it's the cutest thing I've ever seen. Pop pats Ziggy's head and then Joss says, "Off," and Ziggy drops his paws to the floor. Pop hands him a treat and a little drool gets on Pop's fingers when Ziggy eats it.

"Good boy," Pop says, but he sounds sad.

"I'll find it," I tell him. "Don't worry. Why don't you finish telling the story? I'm sure it's just in your room somewhere. I'll be right back," I say. I head for the stairs.

"Joss, why don't you keep her company?" Grandpop suggests. "Would you mind?"

"'Course not," Joss says. When she comes up behind me, Ziggy follows. "No, Zigs, I'll be right back. You stay, okay? Ike, can you give him another treat?"

Pop nods and Ziggy turns as soon as the other residents call him back. I hear Pop say, "So yeah, where was I?"

Mimi says, "You were both going to walk across town," and I

can see Pop's smile return though it's definitely a little dimmer than it was before.

I look at Joss. She smiles too. I feel fidgety because she's so pretty, but I still want to know her.

I swallow hard and smile back. Then we both step away from the sunlit room and into the dark.

Her bracelets are a riot of bells.

I turn on the flashlight on my phone so I can see where I'm going on the shadowy stairway, and so I can check the stairs and floor along the upstairs hallway for the picture. Even though I don't look back, thanks to Joss's bangles, I can hear that she's there.

"Pop's room is right down the hall," I say once we get to the top. "I bet the picture just fell out of his wallet in there."

"No worries," she says. "I'm happy to help you look around."

I push open his bedroom door and step inside. I yank at my denim skirt because my minis always ride up when I climb stairs. It's slightly brighter inside his room than it was in the hallway, maybe because the walls are closer out there. His only window faces the brick wall of the house next door, so though the sun still shines, long shadows paint the floor.

I prop my phone up on Pop's desk, and Joss does the same with her phone on his dresser. The two beams cast a soft white light through the dim room. My grandfather left a sweater thrown over the arm of his lounger, and his bed is unmade, but otherwise the room is pretty neat. In the center of the floor there's a blanket spread out with small packets of snack crackers and chips on fancy china, a ceramic teapot, and cups with the leftover dregs of tea. I blush, a little embarrassed, when Joss says, "What's all this?"

"Oh, um." This girl is cute. I am weird. I thought I'd have a little more time before she saw the freak flag I'm always trying to hide.

"We have vending machine tea party picnics sometimes," I say quietly.

"Vending machine . . . tea party . . . picnics? But, there's no vending machine in Althea House, is there?" Joss asks.

I kinda cringe, still facing away from her. "No," I say. I move the blankets around on Pop's bed like I'm looking for the photo but I'm mostly just trying to not look at her. "I grab the snacks from the vending machine at my job – I'm a lifeguard at a YMCA – and bring them with me when I come visit Pop."

"What?" Joss asks. It sounds like she's smiling, but I don't turn to check. "Why?"

"It's dumb," I say.

Joss taps me on the shoulder, so then I do turn around. She's smirking at me and she's so beautiful, even with shadows falling over her face. She's frowning a little too, like she's confused.

"Nella."

It's the first time she's said my name, and the way it sounds in her voice makes me feel even hotter. I blush more, grateful for the closeness of the room and my own dark skin. I don't think she can tell.

"It's just this thing. We used to do it with Granny Zora when she was in the hospital. You know. Near the end."

Joss shakes her head, not really getting it, so I keep talking.

"Tea parties and picnics were her two favorite things. She couldn't get outside anymore, and she hadn't hosted a tea party since she'd gotten sick. So one day I got this idea. I picked up her favorite china from their apartment. I told Pop and my mom to buy a crap ton of snacks from the vending machine, and we spread them out on her hospital bed and had this combination tea party picnic. It made her so happy and cheered the rest of us up too. So now sometimes when I'm sad, Pop will tell me to 'bring reinforcements.'" I gesture to the floor. "He's always talking about this."

Joss smiles. "Oh," she says. "Oh God. That's real adorable."

I blush harder.

A moment later, she starts crawling around on the floor, moving the china and blanket gently aside. I realize she's looking for the photo and remember that's why we came up here in the first place. Then I'm pulling open drawers and lifting my grandfather's sweaters and socks, trousers, and T-shirts. But I don't see the photo anywhere.

"My Nan died a couple of years ago," Joss says quietly. "She was a show dog trainer. Like, those women who run with the dogs across the blue carpet while they do tricks?"

I smile a little and nod. "You don't see many Black people doing that," I say.

"I know," Joss agrees. "But she was real good at it. Every

dog she ever trained was Best in Show at some point. Then, when she got older, she started training therapy dogs. It was a little less physically demanding, but she still got to be around animals all day."

I think about Ziggy and ask, "Did she train your dog?"

Joss shakes her head and pushes her glasses up her nose. "I did. But she taught me everything I know."

"How long did it take?" I ask her. I pull out the last of Pop's drawers and push everything inside around.

"A few months. I adopted Zigs when he was like one-ish. He was this buck wild puppy. But he was so sweet and cute. I could tell, from seeing the dogs my Nan had worked with, that he had the right temperament to be a therapy dog. I couldn't understand why no one had adopted him sooner."

"A lot of people think pitties are scary," I say. "There's a lot of dumb stuff on the internet."

"Oh, I know. It makes me so mad. Did you know that pitbulls are the most euthanized breed? And that black dogs, regardless of breed, are the least likely to get adopted?"

I shut the drawer and turn to look at her. "Really? Damn," I say. "I didn't know that. It's almost like . . . dog racism."

Joss shakes her head. "That's exactly what it is. But anyway, Ziggy took to the training right away. Very eager to please. Very gentle. Very stranger-friendly. We started out visiting kids at the hospital and then started going to old people's homes. I make hospice visits once a month with him, but I can't do those too often for my own mental health."

Joss stands up and lifts a stack of books on Pop's bedside table. Then she flips through them all one at a time, which I hadn't thought to do. Photos do make great bookmarks.

"This her?" Joss says, and for a second I think she's found the missing picture. But when I look up, I see that she's pointing to Sadie's painting of Granny Zora that's hanging by the bedroom door. I smile a little.

"Yeah," I say.

In the portrait, like in the photo, Granny has all her long gray hair pressed straight, but it's falling over her shoulders in fat waves because she always pinned it up before bed. She's wearing an emerald-green dress and sitting at her kitchen table with her elbow resting on the tabletop, and she's holding a cigarette, the very reason she ended up with the lung cancer that took her from us. She looks beautiful and badass and too much like Mom. I turn away.

I feel panicky sometimes when I stare at pictures of her for too long, because I realize that one day my mom's gonna be gone too.

"She's gorgeous," Joss says, and something about the fact that she says it that way, in the present tense, makes my heart slow down, my breath even out.

"Yeah," I say again. "She is."

"You look like her," Joss says. And I blink a few times too quickly.

"I do?" I ask.

"Yep," she says, but she isn't looking at me anymore. She's leaning over, checking under Pop's bed. Still, her voice rings as loud and clear as a pair of her bracelets chiming when she adds, "You're gorgeous too."

I want to tell her that I've been thinking the same thing about her since she first stepped foot in Althea House, but I can't find my voice.

So I don't say anything back.

We search around for a while longer. I shine my flashlight under the dresser and into his closet, and Joss pulls the cushion out of Pop's chair to check the back and the sides of the lounger. But we don't find the photo.

"Did Ike go anywhere else in the house? I mean besides, like, the bathroom and stuff. Oh, what about Queenie's room?"

"Oh yeah," I say, glancing at Pop's saxophone where it sits on the floor in its case. "They're always playing music together."

"I know," Joss says, grinning. I want to ask how she knows, but I don't.

A minute later we're back in the hall, heading to the opposite end of the floor.

"Why were you sad?" Joss asks as we pass the bathroom. I poke my head in and glance at the tile floor, but nothing's there.

"Huh?" I say.

"You said Ike told you to bring reinforcements because you were sad. That's why you had the picnic?"

"Oh, right," I say, remembering.

"What were you sad about?"

I fluff my puffy hair.

"Honestly, I've been pretty bummed since the last day of

school," I say. "My girlfriend went to Haiti for the summer, but she didn't tell me until the day before she was leaving."

"Yikes," Joss says. "Long distance is hard."

"What?" I ask, and then I realize my mistake. "Sorry. My girl space friend."

"Oh."

"Yeah. I . . . actually had a pretty intense crush on her. And when she told me she was going, it was very much like, 'You're needy as hell. I'm going to a foreign country to get away from you. Bye.'"

"Ouch," Joss says. She looks uncomfortable and I'm worried I've said too much.

"I mean, that's an oversimplification, but we were just different, you know?" I yank at my skirt again – a bad habit I haven't added to my list of vices simply because, as Pop has no trouble telling me, I could just get longer skirts.

"Different can be killer," Joss says, and she reaches for Queenie's bedroom door.

I feel a little weird stepping into Queenie's room without permission. I pause, backtrack, and shout down the stairs. "Queenie, you mind if we check your room for the picture? Maybe Pop dropped it in there?"

She hollers back a second later, "Knock yourself out, sweetie. But don't touch my top drawer."

Joss giggles. "I bet she's got porn in there," she whispers, and a second later Aida yells, "That's where she keeps her vintage *Playgirls*!" Joss and I look at each other and burst out laughing.

"Shut the hell up," I hear Queenie say. We step inside so we can't hear Aida's reply, but I'm certain they're still arguing.

I glance around Queenie's room. I take in the patterned floor pillows and lacy curtains, the patchwork quilt on the bed and the stacks and stacks of books about astrology and gemstones and tarot. "It . . . looks like a hippie-ish catalog threw up in here. Except, you know, with less boho white girl energy and more realness."

"Oh my God," Joss says, nodding, "that is the perfect way to describe it."

We scan the floor with our flashlights, and then check behind Queenie's drum set. The old lady rocks out with my grandpa a couple days a week and they've been talking about forming a band, but I doubt anything will really come of it.

"I play the piano with them sometimes," Joss says after we've been quietly looking around Queenie's room for a while. "I bring my keyboard so Queenie doesn't have to carry her drums downstairs. I told them we should form a band, play gigs at the little soul food restaurant on the corner. They have live music sometimes."

"So that's how you knew to check in here. And you're where they got the idea," I say. I nudge her a little with my elbow and she laughs.

"Guilty," she says, then she gets this look on her face that I can't quite read. "Different can be killer," she says, repeating what she'd mentioned in the hall when I told her about Bree. "But I think, no matter how different you are from someone, if you want to make it work and both people are willing to try, you can usually figure stuff out. I mean, look at Ike and Queenie. They're like polar opposites – your grandpa is this super logical, very straight-laced dude and Queenie's room is full of . . ." Joss picks up a big piece of rose quartz from a small shelf and widens her eyes. "But they have this, like, undeniable musical chemistry. Enough that they really want to play together. They argue constantly, but they make it work."

I shrug. "I guess that's true. Aida and Mordy, too."

"Exactly. What I'm saying," Joss continues, "is that different usually isn't the real reason a relationship doesn't work out. It's more about what people really want. And how badly they want it. If someone didn't want you?" She gestures at me with the rose quartz, like something about me is just as precious, just as imperfectly beautiful. "They missed out."

I swallow hard and walk over to Queenie's dresser. "You're . . . sweet," I say.

The part of the Bree story I didn't tell Joss? Days before she left the country, I'd leaned against a fence beside her, held her hand, tucked a lock of her curly hair behind her ear, and whispered, "I don't know if you know this, but I think I love you."

She let go of my hand and took a step away from me. She said, "But Nella . . . you know I'm straight, right?" and I felt my chest collapsing in on itself.

"But we hang out all the time and hold hands," I'd said. "We go to movies together and get ice cream late at night."

"Yeah," Bree agreed. "But I do that with all my friends."

"But . . . Twig saw you kissing girls at all those house parties? That's the only reason he introduced us."

Bree bit her lip. "Oh. Damn. Well, that's just something I do when I'm drinking."

I didn't buy that she was straight. But more important than my issues with how she identified, was my embarrassment: I thought I'd been dating someone who didn't think they were dating me.

Three days later she told me she was leaving. Just like that. On top of the humiliation, I got to add heartbreak – I'd been dumped by someone I'd never even kissed.

So I collect Joss's compliments like shiny pennies found on the ground: pocketed for safekeeping. They're pretty, and nice to have, but worth very little. Because if someone I'd hung out with for months could toss me away as easily as Bree did, why should I care if a cute girl who just met me thinks I'm a catch?

Joss can tell.

"You don't believe me?" she asks. And I shrug.

"Bad things are easier to believe than the good stuff."

She looks thoughtful for a second, then she says, "I just try my best to always say true things. My ex was really different from me too – into metal more than pop. Wore more black than pink. They liked cats . . . Cats, Nella. More than dogs. That bitch missed out too."

I laugh. I've only known her for an hour (if I don't count all the stories Pop's told me about her), but I still can't imagine Joss with someone like that.

She reaches for a tube of Queenie's lipstick and keeps talking. "Taylor was their name. Went by Tay-Tay. Tay was my first, so I'll probably love them forever. But while I wanted Tay just as they were, Tay wanted someone they had more in common with. And you can't make someone want you back."

I knew that all too well.

Joss leaned toward Queenie's mirror and smoothed the color, a deep indigo, over her lips.

"She's let me try this color before," Joss's reflection says when I give her a look. "I swear. I wouldn't use it if I thought she'd mind."

And now, in addition to Joss being very cute and very confident and very kind . . . her mouth is suddenly very, very distracting.

I turn away and remind myself I'm supposed to be looking for a picture, not staring at Joss's lips. I scan the floor and Queenie's bed, her shelf with all the books and stones, and then her side table. There's a jar of butterscotch candies and I reach my hand in and grab a few. Queenie is always handing these out, so like with the lipstick, I know she won't mind us taking some.

I toss one to Joss and sit down on Queenie's bed. "I freaking love these things," she says. She sits on one of the floor pillows, unwraps the candy and pops it into her perfect, purplish mouth. Joss picks up a book from one of the stacks closest to her and asks me my sign.

"Pisces," I say, and then, because she seems so sure of

herself, so unapologetically exactly who she is, I ask, "Did you know, before Taylor I mean, that you were queer?"

"Nope," she says without hesitation. Then she shines her phone light on the page and reads me my horoscope from the heavy book in her hands. It says a few vague things about ambition and transition and leaning on loved ones during difficult times, but I don't really pay much attention to it. I'm watching Joss.

When she finally looks back up at me, I smile. "When did you know?"

"I met Tay-Tay when we were twelve. But we didn't start hanging out a lot until we were in high school. I felt this, like, heat, whenever we were together. We were like magnets. We couldn't keep our hands to ourselves. So you know, we linked pinkies a lot and played with each other's hair and cuddled when we watched movies and were best friends. I didn't really think about it. Then, last year, they came out to me one night. Told me they were nonbinary and queer, and said that they liked me. Tay seemed so sure about everything. I could tell so much thought had gone into everything they said. And I think they could tell I was still questioning. I told Tay I wasn't sure about my identity, and they looked really disappointed. But then I said, 'I don't know if I can tell you which boxes I check. But I know I like you, too.'"

I nod. "It was kind of like that with me too. One of the most popular guys in school, this kid Tristán, gave me a love letter freshman year and when I showed it to my best friend thinking she'd laugh, she told me to go for it. She couldn't understand why I wouldn't at least talk to the guy. But I wasn't interested in him because I had a crush on her. Long story short: she didn't like me back. She got weird about it. I got clingy. We stopped being friends."

"That sucks," Joss says. And we're quiet for a while. I slide off the bed and onto the floor pillow beside Joss. I take the astrology book from her and she angles the phone's light toward me so I can find her horoscope. She's a Taurus and hers is all about opportunity and being open to what the universe sends her way. Her eyes sparkle a little in the dark.

"I don't think the photo is in here," I say, even though part of me wants to stay here beside her for a while longer.

"Nope," she says, but she doesn't move either.

"Maybe we need some help," Joss suggests a few minutes later. She pushes herself up and reaches down. Her outstretched hand is soft when I reach up and grab it. She pulls me up, but doesn't let go right away, and I love the way the cold metal of her rings is such a sharp contrast to the warmth of her palm. We head to the door and Joss's bracelets jangle as she opens it.

"Help?" I ask, following behind her.

She bounces down the stairs and reenters the living room, and Mimi and all the old people look up hopefully at us.

"Sorry, Pop. No luck," I say, and Grandpop Ike says, "Well, shit."

"I have an idea, though," Joss says. "Ike, can I see your wallet?"

"Umm, okay." He pulls it out of his pocket and Joss calls Ziggy over. She holds the wallet out and Ziggy dutifully sniffs it.

"I don't know if this will work," Joss says. "But I'm guessing the photo must smell like the wallet, right? Since it was usually in the wallet? Maybe it smells like the leather. Maybe Zigs can help us search more efficiently."

I bite my bottom lip to keep from smiling too hard. This girl.

"That's brilliant," Birdie says.

"Genius," Mordechai mutters.

"The girl could fight crime," Mimi agrees, without looking away from her phone.

The Costas and Montgomery-Allens all laugh.

"Not without my faithful sidekick. Lead the way, Ziggy," Joss says, then she looks over at me. I'm staring again. "What?" she asks.

I shake my head. "Just . . . you," I say. And I start behind Ziggy. When I don't hear her bracelets, I turn back and Joss is still standing in the same place. "Just me, huh?" she says, smirking.

"Oh my God," I say. I cover my mouth, realizing what I let slip. But when our eyes meet, I decide to go with it. I grab her hand again because it felt so normal to do it upstairs. So natural. "Come on."

Ziggy trots down the long hall that leads to the kitchen, so we follow him through the dim passageway. There are battery-powered tea light candles along the floor in the hall so the residents can make their way to the bathroom if they need to. But the kitchen is bright since there are so many windows.

Ziggy walks over to the sliding glass doors that lead out to a small balcony set at the back of the house. He nudges the bottom corner of the door and leaves a small heart-shaped nose print on the glass.

"I . . . don't think he's leading us to the photo," I say. I slide open the door and Ziggy hops over the threshold, sniffs around, and lifts his leg before peeing a perfect arc through the railing and off the side of the balcony.

"Ziggy, no!" Joss shouts, but it's too late and I'm cracking up laughing.

"Hopefully no one's down there?" I say. I walk to the ledge and peer over. Lucky for us, there's just a spattering of wetness on the concrete.

"Good boy," I say. I pat his soft head and stroke his velvety ears. His floppy pink tongue hangs out and it looks like he's smiling.

Joss says, "That was most certainly not good!"

"At least he didn't pee on the balcony," I say. I flop down in one of the Adirondack chairs and Ziggy pushes his head against my hand until I pet him more.

"They had the right idea," Joss says. She sits in the chair across from me and looks at the building across the alley. The people have pulled out a charcoal grill and they're blasting music from a Bluetooth speaker. Two older men are dancing together and their friends are clapping.

It's weird sitting in the light knowing there are only a few hours of brightness left. I wonder what we'll do, and how everyone will feel, once the sun goes down.

"It's strange to think how we're so used to being able to see everything. I bet it was pretty scary for my grandparents to walk all that way in the dark. Especially with looting and everything else that was happening back then."

"Oh yeah!" Joss says suddenly. "I never got to hear the rest of the story." She pushes her glasses up onto her nose and reaches for Ziggy. He goes to her immediately and climbs up into the chair with her. He's huge and it's hilarious and adorable to see his big body squished on top of hers. "Will you tell me?"

I feel suddenly lonely with the two of them in the same chair, and me a short (but impossibly far) three feet away. I nod and look across the alley again.

"They walked from their building north of Morningside Park all the way to my great-grandmother, who was living in East Harlem, on 116th and Second Ave. And back."

"Whoa," Joss says. I don't look over to see her expression, but I can hear her bracelets and Ziggy's panting. I fiddle with my necklace, a rose gold locket Bree got me for my birthday that makes me more acutely aware of my aloneness, that makes the distance from Joss seem even wider. I drop my hand and keep talking.

"Yeah. But they talked the whole way. She told him stories about growing up in Harlem, because Pop had just moved to New York. He told her what it was like to live in Charlotte,

North Carolina, his hometown, and how glad he was to be up north. When they passed the Apollo Theater, Granny told him her mom had taken her to amateur night and they'd gotten strawberry milkshakes after. She told him how sad she was that the theater had stopped having live shows, and only showed movies now. That's when he told her if the Apollo ever had another amateur night, he hoped she'd let him take her out."

"He had to shoot his shot," Joss says, bracelets singing.

"He did. And then, when they passed an ice-cream truck, he bought her a strawberry cone with sprinkles, and said something like, 'I guess they were out of shakes'. I know Granny loved that," I say, smiling. "And the ice cream must have won her over because a few blocks later, Granny Z reached for Pop's hand when they passed a store that was on fire, and didn't let go the rest of the walk. By the time they made it to my great-grandmother's building, they knew each other's middle names, hopes and dreams, and as Pop puts it, 'that our hands were made to fit'."

Joss sighs a contented sigh. "What's your middle name?" she asks.

"Rose," I say. "What's yours?"

"Mae," Joss says, and then, "My grandparents met at a baseball game. My grandpa was a player, and my Nan caught his foul ball. She asked him to sign it after the game and he wrote his phone number."

I grin. "What about your parents?" I ask.

"They met in college. She was a Delta, and he was a Q.

They met at a step show and swear it was destiny. Yours?"

"High school sweethearts. They got divorced when I was ten, but they're still really good friends. It's weird sometimes. But nice." I smile to myself thinking about how they both came with me to the Pride parade, decked out in matching rainbow T-shirts and shorts. It was so dorky and adorable. "They're cute."

"Ugh, ugh, ugh," Joss says. "I hope I get to experience something like that one day. So damn romantic." And I think sitting here with her, telling love stories, is pretty romantic. I'm about to say as much when my phone vibrates. I pull it out of my pocket and it's her.

Power still out? Where are you?

"Ugh, Zigs, you're on my bladder," Joss says, gently pushing Ziggy off her lap. "Be right back, Nella."

"Okay," I say, wondering if she really has to pee or if she saw Bree's name on my phone's screen.

Against my better judgement, I scroll back through my texts with Bree until I get to the good ones. The mushy, sweet ones we sent each other before she rejected me and left for the summer.

NELLA: I miss your face.

BREE: Not as much as I miss yours.

NELLA: You have the best hair on earth.

BREE: Well your fro is pretty awesome, too.

NELLA: You just get me. How is it that you just get me?

BREE: I don't know, boo.

NELLA: How'd we never meet til now?

More like: How could I have been so clueless?

My chest feels tight with something like longing, something like pain. I scroll down and write back.

NELLA: Yeah, power's still out but it's not even dark yet. I'm at Pop's. I'm good, don't worry.

BREE: Call me. I need to hear your voice to know you're okay.

NELLA: No.

BREE: Why?

NELLA: Because you broke my fucking heart.

I hear the door slide open and I slide my phone back into my pocket.

"I got the wallet from Ike. Let's try this again," Joss says.

She holds the wallet out for Ziggy to sniff, and I sniff at the same time. Dammit.

"Hey," Joss says. She puts her hand on my shoulder and leans over so she can see my face. "Hey, are you crying?"

"Only a little," I say.

"Wait, what? Why? What happened?"

"It's stupid," I say. I rub my eyes with my arm.

"Tears are never stupid," Joss says.

"It's just my stupid ex. Or whatever the hell she is. When we were hanging out, I thought she liked me. Like liked me, liked me. This is so embarrassing, but I actually thought we were dating. It turned out she was just being nice. She just wanted to be friends the whole time but I totally thought something else was going on. Now when she checks on me, it just feels so tainted. Like she sees me as this clueless little kid she has to take care of. It drives me nuts, but I miss her so much that I put up with it. I hate it."

Joss kneels in front of me and uses her thumbs to wipe my cheeks. Except she kinda pokes me in the eye. "Ow," I say. And then I'm laughing.

"Shit, sorry," she says. "Do you need a hug?" I nod and grab her hands so that we stand up together.

We hug. It's nice. She's soft and she smells sweet and fresh, like baked bread or donuts. And because we're the same height, I just fit.

"Now, let's find that photo," she says.

Ziggy's a dog on a mission. He steps back into the kitchen and his nose doesn't leave the floor. He leads us to the basement door, and when we open it, he charges down the stairs like he was born to do photographic search and rescue.

"The laundry room," I say. "Why didn't we think about checking the laundry room?" If the photo had fallen out of Pop's wallet and into his pocket, whichever staffer did the laundry would have probably found it before washing his trousers.

"Ziggy's a freaking genius," Joss says.

There's a battery-powered lantern at the base of the stairs, which Mimi probably left there just in case she needed to come down here to get anything. I pick it up and click it on, and the three of us head back to the laundry room, convinced we're close to solving this mystery together.

I set the lantern on top of the washing machine and we use our flashlights to check the shelving and floor for pocket contents. There are marbles and loose change and keys in little jars all along the shelves beside the washer and dryer. But as we scan each shelf full of receipts and pens and buttons, there's no photo.

"*UGH!*" I say. "I'm so over this. Where else could it possibly be? This place isn't that big. Pop doesn't really go anywhere. It shouldn't be this hard."

Joss is still looking. Her bracelets are making music and Ziggy is following her from one side of the room to the other. She licks her lips, and she's still wearing that lipstick. I'd forgotten since I was avoiding looking at her, trying so hard not to stare on the balcony.

"You don't have to do this, you know," I say. I start to worry she's only helping because she feels bad for me. I think back to everything I've told her and I feel really pathetic. *My granny died. My best friend didn't like me back. I got dumped by someone I wasn't even officially dating*. And then I cried. Jesus.

"I really don't mind, Nella." She finds a laundry basket full of clean clothes and starts lifting the folded shirts and pants, meticulously checking between each article of clothing.

"Joss, stop."

She stops. She looks up at me. Her mouth is so purple.

"It's okay," I say. "You don't have to help me."

"I wouldn't be helping you if I didn't want to help you."

I wince a little.

"Right. That's the thing, though. I think there's something about me that makes people want to help me? Like there's something kinda pathetic about me. I mean, I thought I was dating a girl for two months and even my family members are always trying to help me with my love life. So people want to help, want to take care of me or whatever, but eventually that neediness is what makes them not want me around anymore."

"You don't need to be taken care of, Nella. You're not some helpless little kid."

"I know," I say.

"Do you?" Joss asks, and she sounds kind of mad. "I'm not helping you because you're pathetic. And to be clear, you're not pathetic. You're sensitive. You're soft. You're vulnerable and kind."

I blink a few quick times, my eyes stinging and damp.

"I'm helping you because I wanted an excuse to talk to you, to get to know you, to follow you around this house in the dark. You're . . . kinda amazing. Just like Ike said. But until you realize that, it's not going to matter what I or anyone else thinks."

I'm not sure what to say, so for a long minute, I don't say anything.

"That girl, she probably led you on whether it was on purpose or not, because you're warm and gentle and sweet. She's probably only realizing her mistake now. You're like the rose quartz in Queenie's room: your energy is all love."

I swallow hard.

"I don't know about that," I say, and then I'm speaking faster than I want to be. "You're the amazing one. You trained your dog to help other people. You volunteer at kids' hospitals and animal shelters and old people's homes and hospices. You play the piano like a classical musician, and Pop told me you sing! And I mean, look at you. Your whole . . . being is a freaking work of art."

I hadn't meant to say that last part out loud. But it was true. I'd stared enough to know that. I yank at my skirt.

Joss steps closer to me, and I back away from her until the dryer is right up against my lower back. "Okay," she says, her voice lowering in a way that makes my face warm. "And you came up with a way to keep your dying grandmother happy. You were brave enough to tell your friend you loved her, and you fought to stay friends even when she didn't love you back in the same way. You're still kind to the girl who broke your heart. I saw you texting her. You put out a goddamn fire with nothing but your boot-clad feet! And let's not talk about people being art because . . ." Joss takes a step back, looks me up and down, and says, "Damn, girl."

"Oh," I say. "Yeah, but –"

"But nothing, Nella Rose Jackson."

Up this close, I notice again that we're precisely the same height. And I see that her glasses frames are rose gold, like my necklace.

We match.

Her eyes, on the other hand, are the color of the room we're in – the color of a room with all the lights turned off – but glowing and a little golden in the center like the lantern just beside us. And in here I can see that her skin's a little lighter brown than mine, like the shell of a hazelnut, or the paper towels in the old movie theater bathroom downtown. I reach out and touch one of her long braids, and it feels soft and substantial, like everything else about her is too.

"Okay. Jocelyn Mae Williams," I say. She smiles a little. "Okay. I get it. But the thing is . . ."

"You're afraid," she says. And I nod, thinking about Bree. Thinking about love and how it feels to lose it. Thinking about how much it can hurt.

"I can be brave enough for both of us, if you need me to be," she says. "But something about this, about us, feels special."

I never kissed Bree because I was too afraid. And it feels unsafe and much too soon to let someone new into my shipwrecked heart. But all at once I decide that you can't be brave unless you're at least a little scared.

I look at Joss's dark lipstick, her dark hair, her dark eyes. And before she can say anything else, I swallow my fear and close the space between us.

When we kiss, it's slow and warm. It's thickly sweet, like the butterscotch candy we took from Queenie's bedside table, but there's something underneath the syrupy flavor that I know must be essentially Joss too. I want to taste more of that. I deepen the kiss and I wonder why we've wasted so much time on the opposite sides of rooms, so much time talking, so much time doing anything at all but this.

The first time we break the kiss, Joss says, "We're gonna have to work on your pessimism. Don't you think it's possible that this could be good? That maybe this won't lead to disaster at all? What if we find out that we fit together, like your grandparents and their hands? What if you, with your sweetness and your too-soft heart, those pretty eyes and very short skirts, are exactly what I've been waiting for?"

I blush.

I don't know. I can't know. But I kinda think I want to find out.

I lean in and kiss her more.

The second time we break the kiss, it's me who speaks.

"I cry a lot," I warn her. And she laughs.

"I think I can handle it."

"I text Bree all the time," I say.

"Maybe you should stop texting her and start texting me."

"I didn't want to meet you. I knew this would happen if I did."

"I've been wanting to meet you since the first time Ike said your name," Joss says, and then we're kissing again.

I reach out and place my hand on the part of her belly that I've been staring at since she walked into Althea House. I thank the universe and current fashion trends and God himself for this particular midriff top and the access it affords me. I'm endlessly grateful for whatever lotion she uses because her skin feels smooth and silky. And then she's touching my thighs and I don't care how many times I've had to tug at the denim strip around my waist, I'm so glad I'm not wearing a longer skirt.

I want to kiss and touch her 'til morning, but it only lasts until Ziggy nudges his way between us.

"Not now, Zigs," Joss says against my lips, trying her hardest not to break the kiss for the third time, but when I open my eyes, I see Pop standing in the doorway of the laundry room.

"Pop!" I say. I grab Joss's hand and pull her around so she's beside me instead of in front of me.

"We . . . were going to order some pizza," Pop says, grinning. "Wanted to see if you girls wanted some."

"Oh, yeah, sure," Joss and I both say at the same time.

"You got a little something," Pop says, and he smooths his thumb over his own lips.

The lipstick. It's probably everywhere.

I cover my face and Pop and Joss crack up. Then Joss uses her thumb to rub some of the smeared lip color off my face.

"You still got my wallet, little lady?" Grandpop Ike asks Joss. She tugs it out of her pocket and hands it over. Pop folds it open, and I'm expecting him to take out his credit card or a few bills for the pizza, but he pulls out a small square that can only be . . .

"The photo?" Joss says.

"Where'd you find it?" I ask, not getting it until Pop gives me a look.

"It wasn't . . . ever missing, was it?" Joss asks.

Pop shrugs. "You've been so low, Nella-Bear. And spending so much time here since Bree left. I just wanted you to get to know a sweet girl your own age. I wanted you to make a friend. I didn't think it would develop this quickly. But I ain't mad about it." He smiles more.

I walk over and sock him in the arm. "I don't believe you," I say. But I kinda do.

Ziggy looks from Pop to me to Joss, tail twerking.

"Thank you," I say to Pop, then I rub his arm where I'd punched him and hug him.

"So what kind of pizza do you want?" he asks, turning to head back upstairs. I walk back to the dryer and grab the lantern. I grab Joss's hand too. And I may be high from the kiss and the dark, but I think something about us . . . fits.

"I like Hawaiian, and Ziggy will eat anything," Joss says.

"Pepperoni's good," I say. "But you taste better," I whisper in Joss's ear.

My phone vibrates, and when I pull it out, it's another text from Twig.

TWIG: You gonna get the cups or what????

NELLA: Yeah. Damn. Chill, Twiggy.

TWIG: Aye, what I tell you bout calling me that?!!

I smile, sliding my phone back into my pocket. "I have no idea how we'll get there, but wanna go to my cousin's block party in Brooklyn with me later?"

She smirks. "Obviously. Maybe we can walk like your grandparents did. Get some strawberry ice cream on the way?"

I smile wider, lean over, and kiss her on the cheek.

When we get back upstairs, the residents are whispering.

The Montgomery-Allens grin at us.

Birdie and Pearl lift their eyebrows and then look at each other.

Miss Sadie mutters something about "young love" to Mimi.

Queenie glances at our blushy faces and says, "*Ummhm.*"

Aida and Mordechai are bickering, completely oblivious to us.

There's a gorgeous old lady I've never seen before sitting in the center of the sofa in a fur-fringed robe, holding a glass of wine.

"Well, don't you two look cozy," she says.

"Madame Marie!" Joss shouts, and I say, "Marie? As in *the* Marie-Jeanne Beauvais?"

"The one and only, honey." She squints at us and sips her wine. She pets Ziggy like he's a cat. "Y'all look just like my son did the first time I caught him kissing a boy."

I swallow hard, looking down and away from her. Joss's fingers go still where they're laced through mine.

"Oh, I don't care, little darlings. Not one bit. Love is love, girls. Best you learn that now."

I blush, hard. Joss laughs, loud.

I let out a breath, glance at Joss, and say, "Maybe we should start walking to Brooklyn now?"

Marie-Jeanne hears. "Walk? All the way to Brooklyn? Oh no, sweetpeas. Not on my watch. I'm planning to spend the night at my son and son-in-law's place in Bed-Stuy since my granddaughter and I are flying out of JFK tomorrow morning. You girls need a lift?"

Joss looks at Ziggy. "As long as you don't mind bringing Zigs?"

"Any friend of yours is a friend of mine, hun," Marie-Jeanne assures her.

Joss nods, says thanks, and grins wide.

"Are we ordering pizza or what?" Mordy yells.

And when Joss squeezes my hand, I squeeze back.

THE LONG WALK
ACT 3

Tiffany D. Jackson

Columbus Circle, 7:02 p.m.

We keep walking: down Broadway, past Lincoln Center, straight to Fifty-ninth Street, Columbus Circle. Cars and taxis have been bumper-to-bumper since Seventy-second Street and the circle looks like a parking lot. This city is a hot mess without power. Police tape blocks the Fifty-ninth Street station entrance. Still no trains?

"The trains are gonna be running by the time we make it downtown," I blurt out. "Right?"

Kareem shrugs, not looking in my direction. "Maybe."

"But . . . they'll probably have it fixed soon." Some trains *have* to be working before we make it downtown. They just have to.

"Yeah, right." He chuckles, slicing through the thick crowd on the corner. "Nothing in this city gets fixed quick."

"Ugh! I'm so over this place! It gets a little hot and the whole city shuts down."

"Damn, you really not gonna miss New York at all?"

"Pssh! What's there to miss?" Not with Atlanta and

Hollywood calling my name.

Kareem opens his mouth, then closes it, turning back to his phone as I fan my face. Feels like we've been walking for hours.

"Hey, can we take a break?" I shout.

"Girl, we ain't even to midtown yet! You want to stop now?"

"Kareem, it's hot as hell out here," I snap, sweat dripping down my back. "You can keep walking if you want. But I'm tired, I'm thirsty, and I need a damn break!"

Kareem blows out air and shoves his fists in his pockets. He knows better than to argue when I've hit my threshold. We make our way to a freshly vacated bench near the park entrance. There are a few street vendors on the corner. One selling hot dogs, the other roasted nuts, another phone accessories.

Kareem investigates the table as we stroll by. "Maybe I should buy one of these travel chargers so I can boot up."

"Pssh! And waste all your money? You want to ditch me and my phone that bad, huh?"

He throws his hands up. "Yo, Tammi, it ain't always about you! Some of us got shit to do!"

"Whatever! Do you, bruh! It's your money. Imma be over there!" I don't wait for his reply before storming away to the bench. I can wring out my dress, it's so soaked with sweat. I pull my braids up into a bun and check my phone. Sixty-five percent battery life. Kareem's last phone call must have drained it. What'll happen if it dies? He won't have much use for me then. He might even leave me, all for Twig's party. For Imani. I'll be alone. No phone, no money, no way of making it home if the trains don't start working soon.

I dip my head down, sipping up a few deep breaths.

It's okay. You're okay. It's okay!

"Here." Kareem stands in front of me, shoving an icy bottle of water in my face.

I glare up at him.

"You said you was thirsty, right?" he says. "It ain't that fancy electrolyte water but it's the best I could do, and it was three dollars since we by the park with all these tourists, so you better like it."

I don't want to take it. I don't want him thinking I need him for . . . anything. But I already plan to use my last five dollars to catch the train home once we make it to the end of Manhattan. Because the power has to be on by then. It just has to be. And if I don't put some water in my body, I'm going to pass out from heat-stroke.

"Thanks," I mumble.

"You, uh . . . you not about to have one of those, um, panic attacks again? Right?"

My cheeks catch on fire. I turn away to sip my water.

"Nah," I mumble. "Just hot, that's all."

That was a lie. A tremor has been building in my chest, threatening to erupt since the lights went out, and I've been too shook to say anything. Too embarrassed to tell him that I need him and that . . .

No!

No, I don't need Kareem.

I've been doing fine all on my own, with no help from him these last four months.

Kareem doesn't look like he believes me but doesn't say anything either. He eases into the space next to me, sipping his own water, taking in the scene, and I ache with dozens of nosy questions to ask. Where is he going to school? Who does he keep trying to call?

Wait a minute!

Trying to play it cool, I dig into my bag and flip to the call log. I know I shouldn't be doing this. It's like, invading his privacy, but I just have to know. I'll feel better once I do.

It's a 718 number, possibly a landline. Maybe it's Imani's house phone. Who else could it be?

"It's kinda crazy seeing all these people out like this," Kareem says, watching some old man still in his Comcast uniform, trying his best to direct traffic. "You realize we sitting in the middle of this major . . . moment. Like, we gonna be able tell our kids we lived through this!"

"Why you acting like it's World War II?" I laugh. "It's just a blackout."

"Yeah, but some wild things happen during blackouts," Kareem says while checking his phone again. Thought he said it was dead? "You remember all that stuff about the 1970s blackout, right?"

We learned about the 1970s blackout in our New York History elective. Lasted only around twenty-four hours, but enough time to do some major damage in the city, setting off a massive crime spree. No wonder he wanted to get back home before dark.

"Yeah. I remember."

"What if," Kareem says, with a small grin, "that happens again tonight?"

"What? They were burning buildings down! Robbing stores. The Bronx was on fire!"

Kareem laughs. "But after all the looting, that's when they discovered hip-hop."

I raise an eyebrow, lips pursed.

"Yo, I'm serious!" He laughs again. "Clearly, I was the only one paying attention to that documentary you *made* us watch."

"Whatever! They say educational television is one of the best ways to keep your mind sharp for college. Plus, there's only so much of that anime stuff I can stand. I plan on making serious films. The kind that win awards and everyone writes articles about."

He rolls his eyes. "Anyway . . . if it wasn't for that blackout, those dudes wouldn't have stolen those turntables. And then they never would've had all them parties. And we wouldn't have hip-hop today. So . . . maybe something good will come out of all of this like that one did. That kind of magic only happens in the dark."

We catch eyes and I'm itching to lean into him. Just for a moment. Just to feel safe . . . but stop myself, face burning.

"Um. That blackout lasted over twenty-four hours," I say, checking the time.

"Don't sweat it. We'll be back home way before then," he says, standing.

That's exactly what I was worried about.

He glances at his phone for the billionth time, brow furrowed.

"Yo, why you keep looking at your phone?" I ask. "I thought it was dead. That's why you need mine, right?"

He groans. "It's on two percent. And why are you breathing down my neck?"

"I'm just looking for honesty, that's all."

His eyes stretch wide. "Honesty? What you trying to say, I'm not honest with you?"

I shrug. "I didn't say it, you did."

"Yo, I never lied to you. Not once!"

"You did about that party."

"Are you serious? Is that what this is all about? Still?"

"I'm just saying, if you trying to call *her* – you know, the one you just happen to get with seconds after we were done – then just say that!"

Kareem throws up his hands. "You know what? Fuck it. I ain't gonna let you paint me as some dude who lied and cheated on you. But since you being all nosy, then fine!" He takes a deep breath. "I'm calling G-Ma's retirement home. There, you happy now?"

"G-Ma?"

"Yeah. She's afraid of the dark. Ever since–"

"The blackout," I finish his sentence, squeezing my eyes shut. *Damn, of course!*

"Yeah! And my moms got the twins so there's no one to go check on her but me. She's all alone and I don't want her thinking we forgot about her! That's why I'm walking fast. Need to check on her before tonight's party."

His grandma was in the 70's blackout. That's why he was so interested in all that stuff.

Damn, he's supposed to be the one with the bad memory, not me.

G-Ma used to babysit us after school when we were little. She didn't like us being alone, even for a few hours. She'd make up all kinds of games to play after we were done with homework, so we weren't glued to the TV. And when Mom came home from her shift, G-Ma wouldn't let me walk home alone, even though I lived four houses down. She'd always walk with me, making Kareem and me hold hands so we wouldn't get lost.

She must be so scared . . .

"Okay, just . . . hang on a second," I say, and step aside, pulling out my phone. "Hey, Mom."

"Hey, baby. How you holding up?"

"I'm . . . okay. Listen, um, can you do me a favor? Do you think you can stop by G-Ma's retirement home? Kareem is really worried about her. She's afraid of the dark."

"Oh. Uh, sure, okay. I'll try to stop by and give you an update." I hang up and walk back over to Kareem, who's kneading his knuckles into his palm.

"My mom is gonna stop by the retirement home."

His mouth drops. "What! Really? She'd do that?"

"Yeah. Why not?"

"'Cause we not . . . together."

I shrug. "Just 'cause we're not together doesn't mean I don't know how important G-Ma is to you."

He nods, face unreadable. "Oh. Well . . . thanks?"

"No problem."

We stare at each other for a few beats until he averts his eyes and clears his throat.

"Um. Uh . . . so we should take Broadway."

"And bump into all those people in Times Square? Nah, we should walk over to Eleventh and take it all the way down."

"You want to walk through no-man's land in the middle of a blackout? Nah, we ain't getting robbed today."

I bite my lip as his patience thins. "But –"

"Look, can you just trust me? For once?"

"What that mean? I trusted you."

He shakes his head, silently walking away.

But I follow.

There's mass chaos, just as I predicted, as we reach the city's center – the place where everyone comes to see the ball drop on New Year's Eve or to gaze up at all the massive glowing billboards. This time, people are standing around with their phones arched to sky, catching a glimpse of a rare sighting: Times Square gone dark.

"Whoa," Kareem says, laughing, as we move through the crowd. "Yo, I ain't never seen it like this! Look, all the screens are black! This is mad dope!"

I breathe through the motions as I follow, pushing past elbows, hopping over strollers, and side-stepping around those red metal folding chairs the city scatters throughout Times Square for tourists. Most of them are using the chairs to stand on, flashing pictures in awe.

Kareem stops in a small clearing near the Broadway ticket booth in front of the glass bleachers that usually glow bright red. Kareem brought me here once for Valentine's Day because he knew how much I loved being sketched by a street artist. He even bought me roses. Wonder if he remembers that . . .

Cut it out. He never remembers anything.

"Shouldn't we be going?" I ask, itching to get out of the crowd. Too many people, not enough air.

Kareem gazes up with a smirk. "See, girl, that's your problem. You don't know how to live in the moment."

"Huh? Yes I do!"

"Since first grade, you were always worried about what comes next," he continues, still looking up. "Wondering what we'd have for lunch before we even finished breakfast. All of middle school was about which high school we'd go to and all of high school was about college. You never enjoy what's right in front of you."

He looks down at me and smiles. The type of smile that used to melt me. Now, the feeling is . . . uncomfortable. Because that smile doesn't belong to me anymore.

"You're the one who's been pressing me about getting to that party on time," I snap.

"Yeah but we're, like, living in the middle of history. Stuff like this only happens once in a lifetime and you won't take a second to just. Look. Up."

He places an index finger under my chin and tilts my head back. The sky is a deep blue and we're swallowed by skyscraper shadows. Any other day, standing here would be like sitting inside a light bulb. But tonight, every billboard, every light and marquee, is off and you could almost feel the whole world spinning slow. It's like we're standing in the middle of the universe, waiting for the big bang.

"Whoa," I mumble.

"Told you! Wild, right?"

I can feel a smile take over my face as we laugh together.

"Man, I don't know why you trying to leave early and go to school all far away. Ain't no place in the world like our city. You know you gonna miss it."

I press my lips together, smile fading. "No one's gonna miss me."

"Who told you that lie?"

I blink, neck snapping in his direction. "What?"

The passing headlights dash across his face as he remains silent, his expression unreadable. But his lips . . . his lips are calling me and I'm resisting. Mind and heart playing a game of tug-of-war. Because though I want to kiss him, it doesn't change the reality that he's not mine anymore.

"I . . . I have to use the bathroom," I blurt out.

"Ughhh! You can't hold it?"

"Boy, we just got to midtown and we still got mad miles to go! You expect me to hold my piss for *that* long?"

"Damn," he groans. "You want to squat in an alley or something?"

And just like that, he's back to being an asshole.

"There's a McDonald's on 42nd Street," I reply. "Let's just go there."

"Fine, but can we hurry up? It's already past seven-thirty. I told Twig I'd be there by nine and we haven't even made it to the bridge yet."

My breath catches, like the wind got knocked out of me.

It's fine. All the trains will be working by the time we get to the bridge. Don't freak out.

"Well, you the one standing around staring up at some dead screens," I snap, making a sharp turn and colliding right into a man standing on a red chair.

"Ahhh!" the man hollers as he tumbles, and I trip with him, nearly landing headfirst on the concrete . . . before Kareem catches me by my waist and scoops me back up.

"Whoa! Yo, you okay?"

Feet dangling, I glance up at him, then down at his arms, feeling something like vertigo.

"Um, yeah, yeah, I'm fine," I babble, scrambling to unhook myself from his hold. *He's not mine*, I repeat over and over, forcing myself to forget how good it felt to be in his arms again.

"Hey!" the man says from the ground. "You broke my phone!"

He sits with his cell in his palms, the screen shattered. *Yikes!*

"Sorry, I didn't see –"

"Are you blind? You can't see someone right in front of you?"

"Hey, don't talk to her like that," Kareem barks. "It was an accident, so chill!"

The man stands up, dusting off his legs. "So, are you gonna pay for my phone screen or is your little girlfriend?"

Kareem steps in front of me, sizing him up. "Man, I ain't paying for shit. Neither is she."

"Well, one of you has to. You can't just break people's stuff and walk off."

Kareem scoffs. "You've gotta be a tourist, talking like that."

"And it was an accident," I snap and turn to Kareem. "Let's go, this guy is wildin'!"

"All right then, I'm calling the police."

"Bruh, are you serious?" Kareem barks. "Do you hear yourself? We in the middle of a for real emergency. They a little busy right now!"

A crowd starts to circle around us as they argue, phones ready to record anything that's about to go down. We'll be all over social media before the blackout is done. What if our colleges see and kick us out before we even have a chance to start?

"Kareem, let's just go," I beg, yanking at his arm.

"No, you are not going anywhere!" the man says, taking a step in our direction.

"Or what!" Kareem barks in his face. "You gonna try and stop us?"

The man hesitates, as if weighing his options. And Kareem

has no intention of backing down. I've seen this movie before. So I pull a move I used to do in middle school, when Kareem was being bullied by assholes around the block – I hold one of his hands in both of mine and draw him in, closer.

"Kareem," I plead softly. "Please. Let's go."

Kareem blinks away from the man, eyes landing on me. In that moment, we are us again. Words said through the simplest look. And though it's unfair to my already confused heart, it's the only way to keep him focused on me.

Kareem gives a hesitant nod, gripping my hand. The man yells behind us as we walk away, weaving through the crowd. We don't stop until we reach the corner of Forty-second Street and Broadway, only to find the McDonald's closed.

"Damn," I grumble.

Kareem glances down at our hands and releases his, clearing his throat.

"Um . . . there's another bathroom at that big library on Fifth," Kareem offers.

"You think it's still open?"

"They wouldn't shut down the library. That's, like, against the law or something."

"Okay. Let's try it."

"Wait, hold up," he says, pointing to a sandwich board sign posted up on the corner that says Free Ice Cream with arrows. A grin spreads across his face.

"Kareem, no . . ."

But it's too late. He races down the block and disappears

into a packed shop. I wait outside, leaning against a street sign. Even with the sun gone, it hasn't cooled down a bit and there's about a million people out roaming the streets. I'm surprised we haven't all fainted.

Look, can you just trust me? For once?

I can't get his words out of my head. What made him say that? Why didn't he think I trusted him before? And after everything that's happened, didn't he ultimately prove that I was right not to?

"Here we go!" Kareem emerges with two cups. "Cake batter ice cream with graham crackers and strawberries for the old lady. Happy, uh, early birthday?"

"Wow. Thanks," I gush. "You remembered."

"Of course."

We speed walk east down Forty-second Street, past the stores, the restaurants, and Bryant Park. By the time we make it to the New York Public Library, my ice cream is nearly a milkshake.

"Hey, let's finish this before it melts . . . then go in to use the bathroom," I say.

"Aight," Kareem agrees, relieved.

We sit on the concrete front stairs, in between the giant lion statues, looking down at the passing traffic on Fifth Avenue. Seems like the only lights working in the city are from cars, trucks, and taxis.

"Shouldn't we eat something first? Like a real lunch or dinner?" I laugh, popping the plastic top off my cup. "G-Ma would kill us knowing we out here having dessert before veggies."

"What I keep saying? This is history, might as well have our dessert first," he says, digging his spoon in. "Mmm! Even half-melted, it's fire!"

I slip the spoon out of my mouth, enjoying the icy coolness and the perfect combination of ice cream toppings we came up with together one summer. I wonder if he's had this with Imani. Really, I wonder about all the things they do together that we used to.

"My dad's getting married."

Stunned, I nearly drop my spoon.

"What? Really?"

"Yeah," Kareem sighs, shaking his head but smiling. "He's having one of them destination weddings in January. Asked me to be his best man. Surprised your mom didn't tell you. I know her and my mom talked."

Mom's been pretty good about following the No Kareem rule, but this is definitely some hot tea she should've spilled!

"How's your mom taking it?" I ask.

"She's . . . mad. Or, she *was* mad. Then upset. She wouldn't speak to him at graduation. I get it, though."

"And . . . how do you feel?"

He rubs the back of his neck with a sniff. "I mean, at first, guess I just thought . . . you move out, get a new battery in ya back, and put all that new energy into the wrong person. I just wish he tried, like for real tried, with Mom. Not just for her, but for me and the twins. I told him that . . . 'cause what I got to lose, right? Ain't like he can throw me out the house he don't live in."

"Whoa," I reply. Kareem's the last person to say exactly what's on his mind. "What did he say?"

He takes a deep breath. "Said something like, 'People grow apart, people change. And you can't fight change. Fighting someone who's changing is a fight with yourself. You can only accept them and choose to love them anyway. And if you can't do that, you have to let them go, for your own well-being.' I guess I get that. Anyways, we talk now. Like, talk like we bros. He gives me all this advice about . . . stuff. His girl's pretty dope. They travel, taking cheesy-ass photos, working out together . . . they seem like best friends. I'm happy for dude. Kinda wish we were like this sooner. Like, four years ago when he left."

Kareem laughs. And it's good to see him so . . . happy. He and his dad haven't been close since middle school when the fighting started. I try to ignore the gnawing at my stomach, the resentment. I should have been there for him while all this was going on. Not Imani. Which makes me wonder . . . why wasn't I there?

"Did you mean what you said earlier?" I ask. "That you think . . . I broke up with you?"

Kareem slowly takes the spoon out his mouth.

"Ain't that what you did?" he mumbles. "You pretty much left me a Dear John letter in my text."

"I guess . . . well, never mind."

He arches an eyebrow. "Nah, say it."

"I thought you . . . broke up with me."

"What?" he spits. "How? I didn't even say nothing."

"That's just it, you didn't say nothing. You just left me on read."

"So why didn't *you* say something?"

"'Cause!" I stab my ice cream. "You went to that party. Without telling me."

"Yo, I'd been waiting forever for someone to put me on. I thought you'd understand."

I shake my head. "You were just looking for a way out. You always wanted to go to all those parties."

"Yeah! 'Cause I like music! Ain't my fault you don't do crowds."

"And I told you how I felt about that girl."

"And I told you, you had nothing to worry about. I'm with *you*! I mean . . . was."

I take a deep breath. The sting of that "was" hits me right in the throat.

He stands up and starts pacing on a step below.

"Did you even read that trash message?" he went on. "Was me going to that party worth all that fire you breathed? That was my first paid DJ gig! I thought you'd be happy for me. Especially when we always did whatever you wanted. Instead, you called me a fucking liar and cheater when I never *ever* cheated on you or lied! I only made her my girl after you dumped me!"

"For the last time, I didn't dump you!"

"You stopped talking to me! What'd you expect me to do?"

"You could've walked your ass down the block, knocked on my door like you've done a million times since we were kids, and talked to me. That was your job as my boyfriend!"

He stops in front of me and leans forward, digging into my skull with his eyes.

"Tammi, my only job was to love you. You telling me I didn't I do that? You talking about jobs, what was your job supposed to be?"

My heart hiccups into my throat. I don't want to hear this. I don't want to have this conversation. I don't want to talk about love or anything else. It's over! There is no him and me, no we, just him . . . and her.

"We . . . we should get going," I say. "You have that party tonight, right?"

Kareem opens his mouth just as a homeless man sprints up the stairs, passing us. We watch him rush to one of the library doors and yank at it. Locked.

"Shit," we say in unison.

"Now what do we do?" I groan. "I'm not peeing in a damn alley!"

Kareem purses his lips before his eyes trail down to my feet. "Ughhhh! You and these damn laces!"

I follow his glare. So used to them being undone in some way, I didn't even notice.

He kneels down, fingers working fast over the laces.

"Why you even buy sneakers if you can't ever tie them right?" He sucks his teeth with a huff. "Man, what you been doing all these months without me? Probably falling over yourself – surprise you ain't break your damn arm yet."

He finishes tying my left shoe and moves to my right. I flex my foot and instantly, my ankle feels snug, secure, and safe. For maybe the first time in months.

"Thank you," I say, my voice soft.

He freezes, as if the words triggered something inside him. Slowly, he thaws, shoulders relax, hands gently move from my laces to behind my right calf, eyes focused on my shoe. Then, he leans his forehead on my bare shin and breathes in.

I stare at the top of his head, heart pounding. Aching to move, to run from his touch, but desperate to stay in the dark with him like this . . . forever.

He turns his head, letting his cheek rest against my leg.

"What happened to us?" he whispers.

And for the first time, I'm not entirely sure.

ALL THE GREAT LOVE STORIES ... AND DUST

Dhonielle Clayton

New York Public Library, 8:03 p.m.

Some stories are better told in the dark. Not just the scary ones where someone gets chased through the woods. Or the whodunits where a bunch of suspects are trapped in a house. But even love stories can glow when the lights go out.*

I sneak past the Astor Hall doors in the library. A stream of people flood the street, their faces full of panic probably about the coming sunset and how dark the city will be soon. But I can't wait to see it. Two people sit beside one of the building's stone lions, and I can't stop watching them. When I was a little girl, Gran would take me here and we'd greet each one, and she'd whispers that the pair of lions – Patience and Fortitude – protected all the library books from harm. I'd stare up at my smug grandmother, always asking her why anyone would want

---

* The truth: I've never had a love story. Only 1 in 562 people find love. Supposedly. I read that yesterday and added it to my scrapbook on relationships. I cut out the meet-cute and wedding stories they print in the newspaper. But I think finding love is as rare as finding identical snowflakes.

to hurt books, and she'd wink, then remind me that the stories we tell can be dangerous.

The boy leans in front of a girl who looks about my age, her braids as thick as the ones I took out last week and her skin about my shade of brown. I wonder if she has freckles like me. She gazes at the boy strangely as if she has a question to ask him, a question like the one I'm carrying around inside me.

Makes me wonder if there's already a love story between the two of them. Or space for one. And if one day, I could have that, too.

"Hurry up before we get caught." My best friend, Tristán, waves me forward into the Children's Center.

I run behind him as they start to manually close the outer doors and finish closing the library early due to the blackout. The metal screech echoes.

We tiptoe into the darkening room.

"Lana, just say you lost – I'm not trying to sleep here and definitely not missing Twig's party for our bet." Tristán thumps my arm. "I told him I'd emcee," he says in his signature podcast radio voice. "Can't let my boy down."

"It could be like *From the Mixed-Up Files of Mrs. Basil E. Frankweiler*, but like the library edition," I tease. "A slumber party."

"What?"

He doesn't remember how many sleepovers we used to have. How he's been a snorer and sleep talker since kindergarten. "We read it in the fourth grade. Mr. Ahmed assigned it."

"I don't have the kind of memory you do."

I wave my latest scrapbook journal at him. "If you self-reflected more and actually documented things, maybe you would."

"*Or* if I'd been born with genius-level memory like you, elefantita." He tries to touch the retro elephant-print scarf I have tied around my pin curls. Sweat soaks the edges of it and I fiddle with the bobby pins holding it in place. I can feel my bangs start to puff; the perfect victory roll headed for disaster. This retro look isn't going to make it until the party. Bad idea. July ruins outfits. I smooth the front of my romper. But I need everything to go perfectly tonight. It has to.

I suck my teeth and pretend to hate how he's called me a tiny elephant our whole lives – all because of my legendary memory that teachers and librarians could never shut up about. It was always a new elephant something with every birthday or Christmas. My room is filled with them. Small reminders of him everywhere, making sure I could never forget. "Do they really have good memories?"

"What?"

"Elephants."

"That's what everyone says."

"Who is *everyone*?"

"You're acting funny."

I kick at him. "Your face looks funny."

"The ladies don't complain." He pushes my leg out of the way. "Too scrawny! Don't even try it."

I sideswipe him as we investigate the room. He turns on his flashlight app. The glow of it makes his dark skin perfect. We are giants weaving through all the tiny chairs and tiny tables. The scent of the heat wave creeps inside, mingling with the library smells of paper and ink and dust and glue. Almost like everything is sweating, if that's possible. "I'm not done yet," I say, ducking down another aisle of books.

"Pay up. I win. Let's call it. We need to get to Brooklyn. Twig's waiting." He glares over the bookshelf at me, triumph tucking itself into the corner of his mouth. "You took too long."

"The party doesn't start until like ten anyways. We've got plenty time." I run my fingers over the tiny book spines. "You're trying to run down the clock. You're scared." I stare back at him even though he can't fully see me.

"The clock is done, yo. We went to *three* bookstores and now we're here about to get stuck in the library, and you still haven't picked anything." He chases behind me. "And you've been too quiet."*

"I guess you can't *hear* me talking to you right *now*." I round the corner and cut off his path, reaching up to shove his shoulder. He's so much bigger than me. Last summer he was looking directly into my face, his deep brown eyes always full of

---

* The truth: I have something to tell you. And I don't know how, so I've been lying. When Dad does his whole therapy talk, he says people lie for three reasons: (1) Because they fear the negative consequences of telling the truth, (2) Because they want other people to believe something about them that isn't true, and (3) Because they want to avoid hurting someone's feelings. But what happens when those feelings are yours?

challenge, and now he's a whole foot taller.

"You know what I mean," he says.

"I don't . . . so enlighten me."

He circles me. "Something's up. Spit it out."

"You're paranoid." I turn away from him.

My phone lights up.

Another text from my other best friend, Grace. She's asking me if I've told him the *thing*.

I can't. The words are all jumbled up inside me.

"Is this because you're leaving? Everything will be here when you get back."* He pulls a few more books off the shelves, sets his phone upright so the light beams down on them, and thumbs through the pages. "I'm supposed to help you and your dads move you into your fancy-ass Columbia dorms before I bounce to Binghamton. Relax! I can feel you tripping."

"I'm not," I lie. "Stop distracting me. You're a cheater."

"Fine, ask for a redo. I know you want to. I'm ready for all the whining. Blame the blackout, Lana."

"Shut up. You're already getting all butthurt. You're just scared I'll win."

"*I* usually do."

"Let you tell it," I spit back. "Stay lying."

"You ever get tired of trying to beat me?"

---

* The truth: But will you? Or will you find another girl who fills the space I leave behind? Your memory is so bad. Not episodic like mine. Will you remember everything the way I do? Will you replay it like I do? What happens when we both leave?

This is the game between us. Always a bet about who can do whatever thing the best.

At six, when his family moved into the brownstone next door, he knocked on my door and said, "Bet I can ride my bike faster than you can."

Not *hello* or *hi* or even *hola*. Not *We're your new neighbors* or *We just moved here from Miami*. Nope. He just handed me the tres leches cake his mother made and challenged me.

At eleven, he almost drowned at the Kosciuszko Pool after saying he could hold his breath the longest.

At fourteen, he could watch the scariest horror movies ever made back-to-back but would lie about having to sleep with the lights on.

And today, at eighteen, it's *this:* What's the best book ever written?

But whenever he loses, he twists the whole thing to make himself the winner. That's really his favorite part. There's always a story that lingers long after the bet.

Tristán lives for the shit-talk.

I clutch my scrapbook journal tight to my chest. The pages threatening to expose themselves, the fragile rubber band barely holding it all together.

"Stop trying to cheat." I hold my phone up, the light beam washing over thousands of tiny spines, as I move to the back of the room. I try to focus. I try not to let him get into my head. I try not to get distracted by everything I promised myself I'd tell him today.

"We gotta get back to Brooklyn. Twig's been sending me mad texts." He flashes his phone screen at me. There is a flurry of notifications, some from Twig and some from different girls sending heart and smiley face emojis. "He keeps saying I'm not there for him anymore."

Tristán's dad moved him and his sister to the Bronx at the beginning of the summer. After Mami died last year, they couldn't keep up with the bodegas and needed to be closer to his aunties and grandma so they could help with little Paloma. Now, we meet here. Halfway between Bed-Stuy and Mott Haven. But everyone in the old neighborhood misses him. He's the type that leaves behind a gaping hole.

"You still have my mic at your house?" he asks.

"Yes, for the hundredth time." His podcast equipment is still tucked under my bed where he left it. "But a bet's a bet."

He flashes his phone light over the murals ringing the room, colorful images of New York City brought to life with bright wallpaper.

"You *really* going to pick a kiddie book?" He pulls back his locs into a ponytail. "That's your idea of the best book ever written?"

"Children's books are the reason you even like to read." I scan the shelves for *Mufaro's Beautiful Daughters* by John Steptoe, or maybe I'll grab *Honey, I Love* by Eloise Greenfield or *The People Could Fly* by Virginia Hamilton. I was made for this challenge. Papa is a famous author, his books on politics and race relations sit in every bookstore window, and Dad is a therapist who uses books to unlock people's struggles. Plus, Gran used to read to me on summer nights like this one. We'd curl up in the nook of my bedroom window with my younger brother, Langston, and in between the page turns, she'd complain about the city noises and how much she missed her little library in Haiti from when she was a child.

My last name shouldn't be Beauvais. It should probably be *Livre* or *Mots* or something that translates to *books* or *words* or *story*.

He won't beat me. "Show some respect."

"Not gonna win." He bites his bottom lip and clutches his book bag to his chest where he's hidden his pick. "We should get out of here in like thirty minutes. The trains aren't running and the ride apps are backed up. I just looked and it's a forty-eight minute wait for a ride. So we need extra time."

"We aren't going to miss the party. Chill," I say.

"We can't be last minute with the trains not working. You gonna remember the time, elefantita?"

"Of course." It's just a party, I want to say.

"You better. I can't miss it just 'cause you're being all weird and shit and feeling like you're over high school."

"You're wack. I don't even like you."* My heart is doing a weird flip-floppy thing and I can't seem to calm down. All

---

* The truth: I don't know how I feel anymore. I fill my scrapbooks and bullet journals with my feelings: magazine clippings of confusing words, ink stamps, thick paint swirled around the pages. It all mirrors my mind and its ramblings. Papa says writers need to unlock their feelings in order to tell the truth on the page. But what happens when it's not the page you're pouring your heart out to, when you have to say the words out loud?

the memories crowding in my brain. All the worries about what happens when we can't spend the summer together. All the fears about what happens next year when we're in two different places.

It's making my brain foggy. I can't think through our latest bet, can't figure out the strategy to beat him.

This wasn't how I imagined the night would go.

It was supposed to kick off a new scrapbook. A new set of memories. A new set of the most amazing moments to replay in my head over and over again. A new set of pictures to draw and collage around my words.

I clutch the old scrapbook to my chest again, the edges slick from my clammy hands.

Gran said this is a summer of new stories. Adventures. Magic. Even romance. That the City of Light would teach me about myself, give me extraordinary firsts, help me find a story to write. That Paris would offer me enough to fill a hundred scrapbooks. That she had unfinished business there and she'd show me how to finish the things one starts.

This trip . . . this summer feels like one where everything will change.

But now, stuck in this dark city and this dark library, I wonder what that will mean for us.

"So what time should we leave then, elefantita?" he asks.

I rattle off exactly what he told me *and* tell him how long I estimate us getting from Bryant Park to Bed-Stuy, given the usual traffic patterns made a mess by the blackout.

He scowls at me. "Glad you remember."

I scoff. "You're pressed."

"Or try *responsible*," he replies.

"Okay, Mr. Responsible."

I can feel his smile.

"What?"

"I think I want you to buy me new headphones. Need ones that'll work better with my mic. That'll be my prize." He thumps my shoulder. "A good parting gift for our last summer bet." He tries to peek at the books I'm pulling from the shelves. "Since you're leaving me here and all."

"You mad?"

"Who am I going to argue with while you're gone?"

"Keisha."

He sucks his teeth and corrects me: "Kelly."

"Oh, excuse me. Let me make sure I get all of their names right."

"Stopped talking to her last week."

"Not smart enough? Oh, wait, no, let me guess – bad breath or snaggletooth?" My pulse races. There's always a girl chasing Tristán Restrepo. They come and go, one after the next. He's the smartest, the tallest, the most charming boy on the block. Well, used to be on the block, used to live in the brownstone next to mine, used to be waiting for me every morning. He's always been my shit-talking neighbor – and best friend. But I don't know what we'll be as we spend the summer apart and go to different schools in the fall.

"She doesn't have enough to do. Always waiting on me." He

sighs. "But back to the bet . . . if you happen to win – which is unlikely – what do you want? I'll have to grab it before you head to the airport tomorrow night. Everything is probably closed now because of the blackout."

"What if it's not something you buy?" I almost whisper.

"What?"

"Not telling you yet."*

I can almost hear him thinking, trying to puzzle out what I might want. He's always so arrogant, believing he knows what I'm about to say.

"I'll grab you a gift card to that spa you always talking about. To get your mustache waxed."

"If I got a mustache, it's more than you got." I pucker my mouth at him and put the books back on the shelf.

"Freshen up those eyebrows, then. Or tattoo them on."

"What do you know about eyebrow-tattooing?"

"You know Magdalena Cruz? She was in Calc with us last year. She got them shits."

I look up at him. "How would you even know that?"

He grins. "Guess."

I roll my eyes.

"The new girl I just met is part Guyanese. She gotta get them done weekly. Eyebrows for daaaaaays."

---

* The truth: I don't know if I can say the words out loud just yet. Even though our family rule is: *There are no mind-readers in the Beauvais-Simmons house.* So words and feelings tumble out over cornbread and tchaka. But I don't know how to do that now.

My heart tightens. "Another girl. Of course."

"Can't help it if the ladies love me. I'm popular. She cool though. You'll like her. She's friends with Seymour's cousin."

"Whatever."

"Whatever, what?"

"You always have a crush."

"Big heart. So much love –" He sticks his tongue out at me. "– to give."

"While I'm gone, you'll bump into a girl and next thing I know, your nose'll be as wide as the Lincoln Tunnel. You'd sell your whole house to make a girl happy."

"Everything but Mami's picture." He lifts a picture locket from under his tank, kisses it, and does the sign of the cross. "But you never like anyone."*

Tristán pats his backpack where his book lies. "Just surrender, champ." He puts his warm hands on my bare shoulders. It sends an unexpected shiver through me as if they're suddenly different from the hands I've known my whole life. The same hands I've had endless rock paper scissors wars with. The same hands that dunked me in the pool. The same hands that turned clammy while clutching mine during horror movies. The same hands I held when sitting with him day and

---

* The truth: Because I don't know how to let myself. It wasn't always this way. How do you like someone so easily? Let your hard parts soften up and hope they won't be bruised? I've wondered what this type of *real* love feels like. Another person's hand entwined with yours. Another person's mouth pressed to yours. Another person who wants to be all tangled up with you.

night at the hospital while watching his mother die.

But it all feels so different. Like there will be a before and an after I've said the *thing*. Like there's no going back after the words come out. Like this will be the fissure in the permanent memory of us – a what we were and what we will be.

Tonight it feels like a new story between us.

"Not so quick . . ." I grab his shirt and pull him out of the room. "Book the Ryde, and by the time it gets here, I'll be done."

"Where we going now?" he complains as I drag him from the ground floor up the stairs to the first floor. "Ryde says twenty-eight minutes."

We duck around in the dark. The tinkling jingle of my jewelry echoes. I shouldn't have worn so much tonight. The white marble arches of Astor Hall curve above us. Tiny balls of flashlights dance on the ceiling, and it feels like we're trapped in a great big cave.

"It's beautiful, isn't it?" I glance up even though I've seen it more than a thousand times. But never like this. I might love it even more in the dark.

I remember how the noises of people moving around would echo through the hall. The quiet is beautiful.

"You about to see all type of marble. Arches and stuff in Europe." He makes a snoring sound.

"You have terrible taste. That's why you don't appreciate this. Never have."

"I'm just not into all this bougie shit like you. Our library in Bed-Stuy was never good enough. You'd always drag me all the way here."*

"It's my favorite place in the whole city. You know that."

"I know. I been meeting your ass here these past two weeks."

I don't turn around to scowl at him as I start up the staircase. There are so many stories here. It always felt like maybe all the words in all the books leaked out somehow, seeping into the brass and wood and marble, making the place magic. That it was a place lovers of books came, a place where storytellers and writers were born, a place where nothing mattered but *what if* . . .

"Excuse me. You two – STOP right there!" comes a voice followed by the sharp beam of a flashlight. "What are you doing here?"

Tristán puts his hand up to block the brightness. "Okay, okay." He grimaces and whispers hard to me. "I *told* you this was gonna happen."

"The library closed hours ago. You're trespassing," the red-faced white man says, lifting his phone to no doubt call NYPD.

I step forward in front of Tristán. "Sorry, sir, I left my backpack on the second or third floor. I can't quite remember.

---

* The truth: I just wanted us to have our adventures together away from anyone we might run into. The people we are in Brooklyn aren't the same people we are in Manhattan or the Bronx or Queens. Do you think you can be a totally different person in a different place? Your insides and outsides transforming into another you?

But we've been searching for it everywhere."

"You'll have to get it tomorrow when the library reopens," he barks.

"But it has my wallet and everything in it. My house keys. I won't be able to get home in the blackout," I lie.

He jams his hands to his hips as if exasperated by us. "I'll get it."

"But you wouldn't know what to look for."

"You can describe it."

I rattle off an incomprehensible description.

He grimaces. "I suppose you're right, but *he*" – motioning at Tristán – "can wait with me."

"I need him," I whine.

Tristán holds back a chuckle and I elbow him.

"I'm afraid of ghosts," I add and bat my eyes like I'm helpless and couldn't possibly fumble around in the dark on my own.

A man without pants darts past us all. "What the hell are you doing in here?" The security guard starts screaming and pointing his flashlight. He takes off after the man, leaving us.

We race in the opposite direction, ducking into the empty Gottesman Gallery to hide behind the massive stone columns.

"You're not afraid of anything,"* he says through panting.

---

* The truth: Except for what could come after I tell you this *thing*. I have a closet full of secret fears. If you go into it and push the clothes apart, there's a little hidden door into a little hidden room. I never showed you this, despite the thousands of times you've been in my house. I scrapbook all the things I don't want the light from my bedroom window to find in there. All the feelings I haven't made sense of.

"About to get us arrested."

"You afraid?" I slide my back along the cool marble and sit on the floor. "Turn your flashlight app on again."

He crashes beside me. "I'm not scared."

"Okay." I tug one of his soft locs and he jumps. "Ol' still scared-of-the-dark –"

"Shut up."

"You still got your turtle nightlight?" I pull off my huaraches and let my sweaty feet air out. A blister has started to form on my baby toe.

"Donatello is living his best life. Stop hating." He flinches as we hear a distant noise. "You think there's *really* ghosts in here?"

"Probably. It's where I want to live after I die," I say.

"You said you were gonna haunt me," he reminds me. When we were twelve, Tristán bet me that he could conjure his grandmother through a Ouija board we found at one of those botánica Santería shops. We'd lit all the candles from his mother's prayer altar and sprinkled ourselves with Florida water and sage. We waited for spirits for five hours. I told him none would show up. I won and he had to do my math homework for the week.

But Tristán told the whole seventh grade we met Biggie Smalls that day instead.

They believed him. People always do.

"Let's wait it out to make sure he doesn't come back yet," I say.

"Your feet just hurt."

I wave a sandal in his face.

"Feet stink, too."

"Smell like roses. Best toes ever. Look at that sexy-ass big toe right there. Perfect shape. And my polka-dotted polish is fly." I try to touch him with my foot and he squirms away. "You'd get more girls if you liked feet."

"Or I'd be a creep," he says. "Like what you call those men on the train."

Tristán rode the subway with me to and from school every day, long after we got too big for our parents to take turns dropping us off. His presence, even when we were small, warded off everything on our way from Brooklyn to the Upper West Side.

I sprawl out on the floor. He lies opposite me, our heads beside each other's. One of his locs rubs against my cheek. I don't brush it away. I lift my phone, the soft light finding the glass boxes of exhibits. A poster advertises THE GREATEST LOVE LETTERS OF LITERATURE. I let the light linger over a few poster-sized letters stretched and blown up beneath clear panes. "Remember when you wrote Nella a love letter in ninth grade?"

I can feel his smile in the dark.

"It was the best letter she ever got," he says.

"You wish."

"I'm eloquent."

I couldn't argue with him about that. He could charm his way out of detention or get a grade raised from a B+ to an A-. All the teachers at Stacey Abrams Prep adored him. He would be a great radio host one day.

He starts to read one love letter out loud in his serious "on-air" voice: *"I almost wish we were butterflies and liv'd but three summer days – three such days with you I could fill with more delight than fifty common years could ever contain."* His voice holds a beautiful deep bass. I remember when it had its little boy squeak to it. "Keats knew his shit. This probably made Fanny go wild."

"Maybe."

"You'd die to get a hundred letters like this.* Stop fronting."

"Whatever. Gran got a love letter in May. Well, more like a love email, and then an old-fashioned one arrived. That's why we're going to Paris."

He whips around to face me. "You just telling me? Yo, that's wild. Gran still got it. Been fine forever."

"Shut up!" I swat at him.

"Who sent it?"

"Supposedly a great love of hers. A man she thought she would marry back in Haiti. She was eighteen. Called him her first real love. Said he left for a job in Paris and never came back. And now, one of her best friend's – Auntie Althea's – dying wishes was for Gran to go see him."

"Whoa. Gran 'bout to get snatched up. Granpapa been gone for a long time. Now, her best friend, Althea, is gone, too. She's got to be lonely."

---

* The truth: I'd die to get a letter like this from you. Because my brain would imprint it. Every single word, the way the cursive *e*'s might curl or the *l*'s might loop, would be singed into my memory. I would be able to recite it forever.

The memory of my grandfather's warm brown face filled in: the creases around his eyes, deep wells and tiny smiles, the smell of the pipe tobacco from his shirt pocket, the way his mouth curled as his words slipped from French to Creole and back again. His loss feeling like it happened only moments ago.

Tristán plays with my bracelet. "You good?" I hear the concern in his voice. He came with me every week to see Granpapa as his memories turned slippery, sliding away no matter how many scrapbooks Gran and I made for him.

I nod.

"But imagine having to write a letter every time you wanted to talk to someone. Like how did people really start liking each other or fall in love and shit?"

I roll my eyes. "The art of the love letter is a real thing."

"Nella didn't think so," he says.

"'Cause Nella is queer," I say. "Thought everyone liked you like that."

"They should," he boasts.

"And why is that?" I tease.

"I'm handsome and smart and am a Renaissance man."

I make a vomit sound. I was there when he learned that term three summers ago. His mother had taken us to all the art museums in the city right before she'd gotten really *really* sick. She attempted to teach us both the appreciation of art so that maybe Tristán might take his talent with drawing and painting to the next level. We'd wandered every gallery, looked at every painting or sketch or sculpture, and collected tiny postcards of as many art pieces as we could. He asked so many questions that a docent asked if he planned to be a Renaissance man – a person who wanted to know all the things and have all the talents. He spent the summer trying to do just that . . . and dragging me with him.

"You still can't even spell it," I say.

"Oh, I *can*. I just love *love* and I'm man enough to say it."*

I let my flashlight rest on another blown-up love letter poster. After his mother died, he said his heart would be forever broken. I always thought that's why he didn't like being alone. He was either helping his dad at one of the bodegas they owned, helping his little sisters do this or that, or next door sprawled on my couch . . . or with one of the many girls he kept on rotation.

His phone pings. "Ryde will be here in seventeen minutes, elefantita. Better hurry up."

Panic shoots through me.

"Maybe I should write this new girl a love letter. She's mad old-fashioned. Worse than even Fatima was."

I clench my teeth and try not to let my stomach twist. "Fatima *hated* me."

"She hated anyone closer to me than her. She would've hated Paloma if she wasn't my nine-year-old sister."

---

* The truth: Easy to love. Papa believes people come in two emotional shapes – easy and hard. That there are those who move like water over rocks, cresting, sliding, veering left and right. They don't fight the current. Then there are those who move like mud, full of sediment and rocks and sometimes bugs, and the mud needs added water to unstick itself before moving. I'm mud.

"She would've been your pants if she could. Thirsty-ass."

"Is there anyone still in here?" a voice shouts from the hall entry.

We freeze.

Beams of light cut through the space. "Library is closed."

We wait for the person to walk away before sitting up.

I wiggle my feet back into my sandals.

"You about to lose. Get ready to pay up," he whispers.

We tiptoe on the third floor, passing murals illustrating the history of the recorded world. I used to point and pester Gran with all my questions about how everything came to be. I pull him into the Rose Reading Room.

The arched windows let in the twilight, allowing the room to reveal its treasures: long wooden tables with hooded lamps, bordered by layer upon layer of shelves, red tiled floors with marble paths, and chandeliers. My breath catches as we walk down the long aisle. I remember being a little girl standing in the very center of it for the first time, clutching my bullet journal and pen to my chest, and saying that I would be a writer, that I would have a book that could live here.

Carts hold books. Tristán starts to pause at each one, combing through them as we walk past. "Boring . . ." He lifts one. "Racist." He points to another. "Meh." He pushes a third out of the way.

"Bet the book you picked is *meh*," I taunt.

"You wish. I'll have you know it's hilarious. A great book

should make you laugh. That's part of its job."

"Or cry," I say, walking between the tables. A few personal books have been left behind. I riffle through the pile. It has everything from the books we were forced to read in school to the ones Daddy loves, to romance and weird fantasy. I wonder what this person was researching and why they left all these behind. Maybe they'd be too hard to carry home in the dark? I open the jacket flaps, and spot the same penciled-in name – Eden Shepard. *Why'd you leave these here?*

"Or think." He grabs one of them and waves it in my face. "This how you like your men?" A romance book with a bare-chested white man stares back at me.

I roll my eyes and push it away.

He makes a kissy-kissy noise in my direction. "Get you a white guy like this in Paris? Pierre? Gustave? Pepe? Maybe you'll get your first kiss."

"I've been kissed before."*

"Not a real *real* one. Like a good one." He pretends to hold someone and kiss them. "You get kissed and complain. So those don't count."

"French guys have a reputation. I heard they're good lovers," I boast. "Also, I already speak French."

"When you know Colombianos are the best. You know that."

"Zoraida says y'all are cheating-ass dogs."

"Zoraida is a hater. She had a new boyfriend every week last

---

* The truth: I can't concentrate when kissed. My brain travels to other moments. Ones with him.

year. Almost ended up with two prom dates." He throws the book back on the table. "Remember Chris . . ."

"*Ugh*, here you go."

"You talked to him for all of five minutes . . . and his pants always looked like he was preparing for a flood."

"And all the girls you date are super models out here?" I remind him.

"Nah, nobody said that." He holds up another romance book from the discarded pile and tries to reenact it, holding the bookshelf as if it's some woman. "Romance books can't be the best books ever written," he replies.

"Okay, snob. They're some of the best-selling books ever. Those ladies make money. Gran can't get enough of them. Prolly reads two a week. What if my book turns out to be a romance novel?"

He scoffs. "What do you know about love, anyways? You never have a boyfriend . . . or girlfriend or whatever. How you gonna write about it?"*

"How do you know?" I snap back.

"'Cause I know everything about you."

"No, you don't."

He laughs. "Okay, Lana. This the game we playing today with fifteen minutes left?"

I turn away from him. "Anyways, I'm busy." I run my fingers over more spines. "And I have an active imagination. Enough to write a romance novel."

---

* The hard truth: Because I've been waiting . . .

"You always say that. Never give anybody a shot."

"Why should I? Since you out here trying to play matchmaker." I don't look at him.

"There will be mad dudes at the block party tonight. Everyone trying to holler at you. Last time to shoot their shot before we all leave. Trust me."

"Whatever," I say, trying not to look at him.

"You're afraid of it," he teases.

"I am *not*. It's just so loud." I turn away from him.

"What do you mean?"

"Like my dads. They're so loud. Like their love. You know how my house is." I think about setting my scrapbook journal down but press it to my chest as if the weight of it could slow my heart.

"Your papa and dad are always all over each other."

"Vomit." I suck my teeth.

"Or beautiful."

"Langston hates it, too."

"He's a rising senior now; of course he does." Tristán holds up another book. "They have a great love story. Didn't they meet in a bookstore?"

I brush away the legendary love story of my two dads. Their meet-cute in a bookstore, their whirlwind travels across the world, and the surrogate they hired to happily have my brother and me. Picture-perfect. Nothing can live up to it. Especially not me. That's once-in-a-lifetime type of love. I've visited every bookstore in every single borough of this city, and no one has shown up to convince me. "I just have other things to do."

"Excuses."

"Not everyone needs to be up under somebody all the time. I'm not afraid of being alone." As soon as the words slip out, I regret them. I feel him flinch even in the dark. "That's not what I meant . . . I . . ."

"It is. You said it."

My pulse races.

"You think I'm pressed."

"No, I don't. You're twisting my words."

"It's okay to want to be with people. To like to get to know other people. Not everyone is all right on their own. You out here judging me for it."

"You're putting words in my mouth."

"Whatever." He walks away. The moonlight washes over the annoyed clench in his jaw.

My heart backflips. I didn't mean to make him mad. I didn't mean to push that button. I didn't mean to make him feel like something is wrong with him. This was not how I thought it all through in my head. This was not how I envisioned telling my best friend the truth.

"Then, what is it?" he asks.*

The words won't form. He wanders to the opposite side of the room. Shoulders slumped and fussing with his hair like he does when he's pissed.

Hurry up, Lana, I tell myself. *Pick something. Anything.*

---

* The truth: I think you don't *see* me.

Grace texts again. The same question flashes up at me.

Did you do it?

I abandon my plan of using a romance novel . . . but maybe a good love story might be the only way to try to tell him. My brain toggles through all the possibilities like it's one of those old-fashioned card catalogs probably tucked into one of the backrooms here.

A flashlight cuts through the room. The noise of keys and heavy-soled shoes.

We both freeze.

"Anybody in here?" comes a voice. The security guard.

I hold my breath. Tristán doesn't say a word.

We wait for the sound of the man's footsteps to disappear. I look back at the table of discarded books and jump up. I comb through the pile, finding *If Beale Street Could Talk* by James Baldwin. The book Dad calls one of the great Black love stories. The bittersweet tale of Fonny and Tish, childhood friends who plan to be together, but whose plans are derailed when Fonny is arrested and accused of a crime he did not commit.

My heart squeezes.

"I have it," I call out to him.

"Good, elefantita, the Ryde will be here in eleven minutes."

I hold my breath until he turns around and finds me. The tiniest halos of moonlight dance across the tables and floor. It all feels so weird. The city so dark, so vacant. For the first few hours, the whole place felt trapped under a blanket. Everything a little stiller and quieter, like the city has written a new story for itself. The pen pausing to think for once.

We sit just out of view of the door, finding a beam of light.

"You first," he says, his voice still tight with anger.

"No," I reply. "You can go."

"Nope, might as well do what we always do with our bets."

I sit there, my fingers drumming against the thick book cover, trying to win a gamble that feels bigger than all the other ones combined.

He cradles his backpack and waits. "You had so much to say before but now nothing."

I take a deep breath and hand him the book. He examines the cover then flips to the back. "Papa made me read this," I almost whisper.

"Isn't it a sad story, though? He gets locked up or something. Don't they have to wait to be together?" Tristán's eyebrow lifts with confusion.

"Yeah," I reply. "It's bittersweet. He's taken away for a while, but she loves him so much she is right there by his side. Loving him through that." My voice feels all wobbly. My eyes start to well. I crane out of the light, leaning back into the dark around us so he can't see. I pick up my scrapbook journal again.

He reads the first paragraph of the book and then hands it to me to read the second. The muscle memory of how we used to be when we were little comes back to me, our brown legs tangled together in my window nook. I pause after one sentence – *"I've known him all my life, and I hope I'll always know* *him*" – and look at him.* I start to tell him, but the words get stuck in my throat.

"It's beautiful," he admits. "I remember the story now." He unzips his bag. "You ready for this masterpiece . . . for this brilliance . . . for the best book to ever be?"

"Yes, Tristán," I reply, pushing down the lump in my throat.

"Close your eyes."

"Nope. What are you up to?"

"Just do it. C'mon." He places his big warm palm on my face, forcing my eyes closed. "It's part of the mood. I'm going to read it to you. Its magnificence must be experienced this way."

"Okay, Tristán. You act like you got some James Earl Jones/ Barry White-type voice."

He clears his throat. "You'll eat those words when I'm famous. My podcast will be the most listened to all over the world. Watch."

"Let you tell it." I hear the crinkle of the book open.

"I am Sam. Sam I am. That Sam-I-am! That Sam-I-am!"

My eyes snap open. "Are you serious?"

He grins. *"I do not like that Sam-I-am! Do you like green eggs and ham?"* The big orange and green Dr. Seuss book blocks his face.

I yank it down. "Why are you playing?"

"I'm not. I think this is the perfect book."

I feel my own scowl. "But why?"

---

* The truth: Does he want to know me forever?

"It was funny. Good color palette. I've never forgotten the words to this." He points a finger in the air. "So that's a test of a good book. The rhyme sticks with you."

"Tristán."

"What?"

"Really?"

He puts a hand on his chest. "*Really!*"

"Dr. Seuss drew racist cartoons." I roll my eyes. "Like horrible ones of Black and Asian people. It was bad, bad. He tried to do better, but like . . ."

"Damn, I didn't know that." His voice gets tight and serious. "I don't have time to pick another one." He flashes his phone, where the Ryde app shows the little car making its way through traffic to come pick us up. "So you got this one."

"You're letting me win? We don't do that."

"I would *never* but . . . fine . . . you won." Tristán holds up *If Beale Street Could Talk*.

"Oh, really?"

"Bet. *Beale Street* is definitely better. So what you want? Name your prize. What do I owe you?"

"You're not being serious." I sigh deeply.

"I *am*. C'mon. What do you want?"

I try not to bite my bottom lip as I work up the courage to say what I really want. The heat of his gaze warms my cheeks. I don't turn to look at him. I fixate on the books above his head.

"You're about to ask for something ridiculous and come for

my pockets.* I know it. I still have to get paid. The tutoring gig doesn't pay out until Thursday, and I owe for studio time—"

"I don't want anything that costs money," I almost whisper.

"What?" He thumps my arm.

"Ow!" I rub it and scowl at him.

"What you want?" He forces me to look at him.

My whole body quivers. "I have a question."

"You're playing."

"I'm not."

His eyes narrow. "What is it? That can't be what you want. You just won . . . whooped me, actually." One of his locs falls close to his face and I wonder how long they'll be by the time I get back or if he'll cut them and be a different person when I return from Paris. "You love winning. You can't just want a question."

"That's what I want." My heart knocks against my chest.

"You're acting funny."

"I'm not." My pulse races.

"Spit it out then. The Ryde is about to be here. Twig's still blowing up my phone."

"Never mind." Vomit rises in my stomach. This was a bad idea.

His hand finds my bare shoulder.** "What is it?"

---

* The truth: Some girls want him to spend money on them. They see it as a way to *have* him and prove his love for them. But he would give me the last dollar he had and I still wouldn't want it.

** The truth: Everything feels different now. Even the texture of your familiar hands.

My eyes water. I shake my head and push away the tangle of fear. My feelings start to unravel. "Could you . . ."

His phone pings a thousand times. My eyes cut to all the notifications. He scrunches his nose. "Could I what?"

"Could you ever love me the way you love them?"

Confusion settles on his face. "Who is them?"

I clutch my scrapbook journal tight. "All the girls you're always talking to."

"You're my best friend," he says.

"I know you like . . . love me. But . . . like . . . ?"

His eyes widen – a mix of surprise and I don't know . . . "Oh," is all he can manage.

"Never mind. Forget I said anything."

"That's not something you can just forget, Lana."

"It's cool . . . it's fine." I turn away from him.

He grabs my hand. "Stop –"

His voice gets serious. There's no leftover laughter.

"I don't want to play this game anymore." I'm biting back tears, ready to run out of here.

He pulls me closer. "You don't get to say something like that and run off."

"You don't feel that way about me . . . it's fine. Just let me go. Forget I said anything. I have to go home to pack anyways. I'll see you when I get back –"

"Why don't you kiss me, then?" he asks.

The question is a firework between us.

"What?" I search his eyes, wondering if it's the truth or if he's just being nice. I turn to go again.

He pulls me back. "Just wait . . . say what you need to say."

"I'm scared." My voice breaks.

"Of what?"

"Everything," I whisper.

He takes my scrapbook journal from my hands.

"Don't –" But I don't fight him as he removes the rubber band and lets it spill open, exposing itself . . . and me. Pages chock full of pictures of us and all the things we've done this summer. Movie tickets, menus, photo booth strips, checklists of what we'd planned to do before I left, transcripts of his podcast.*

His mouth opens and closes a bunch of times. Tristán Restrepo, the boy who always has something to say, who has thousands of listeners, who never holds back his feelings, can't find the words. "This is beautiful, Lana." He looks up at me, the brown of his eyes glazing over.

I can't hold his gaze.

"You remember everything." His palm finds my cheek. "Elefantita."

My stomach squeezes.

"I've always loved how your brain works. Remember when we made snow globes in fifth grade?"

I nod, afraid if I speak, I might vomit. This is not how you tell someone you love them.

---

* The truth: Everything we do together is a memory I never want to forget. Each joke, each touch, each experience. My notebooks spill over. Too big to hold all that is him . . . all that is me . . . all that is us together.

A knot twists in my stomach.

He smiles down at our photos. The shape of his mouth is beautiful in the moonlight.

I take a deep breath and square my shoulders. Just spit it out. Get it over with. You can't go to Paris without telling him. "Could you *love me* love me? Or *like* me like that?"

His phone pings, announcing the Ryde's imminent arrival.

This wasn't how I planned this out in my head, not how I wanted it to look all documented in my scrapbook journal, not how I talked it all out with Grace. I wanted to look back on this night and remember how brave I'd been, how clear and confident I'd spoken, how I'd been more like him and less like me in articulating my thoughts and feelings.

"You two!" The security guard stands in the doorway, flashlight blinding us. "Get out of here now."

The security guard walks us to the staff exit. His screams and his threats echo in the darkness, but I can't hear him over the thudding of my own heart.

We burst out onto the street. The street is dark and terrifying. I reach for Tristán, and he reaches for me.

The memories wash over me.

At seven, holding hands on the train platform with our parents on the way to school.

At nine, side by side walking to the hospital to visit Mami when she was first diagnosed.

At twelve, curling our tongues in the mirror as he taught me how to roll my *r*'s in Spanish so I wouldn't fail.

At fifteen, staying up all night as I read him *Pride and Prejudice* so he could write a decent Lit paper.

At seventeen, shoulder to shoulder in front of his mother's grave, watching her lowered into the ground.

The Ryde driver calls Tristán and he directs him to the corner. "You ready?"

"No." I bite my bottom lip to keep it from quivering. I fight away the tears bubbling up inside.

This wasn't the way I wanted to tell him I've been in love with him forever. The way I promised Grace I would say it.

His eyes scan my face. "Of all the things you remember, you can't put two and two together and know how much I love you? How much it's always been you?"

"What?" A tear escapes my eye. "I never thought –"

Before I can finish, his hands are on my back and his bottom lip brushes against my neck, my ear, then my cheek, before he kisses me. His touch stamps out all the worries. His tongue answers all the questions. His warmth is hotter than the blackout heat wave.

He whispers, "I've always loved you, but I never thought you had space to love me back," and kisses me again.

We pause to take a breath.

I can't fight away a smile. "Will you remember this?"

"Forever."*

---

* This will make for a really good story.

THE LONG WALK
ACT 4

Tiffany D. Jackson

Washington Square Park, 8:38 p.m.
We walk down Fifth Avenue in silence, Kareem slowing enough
so it doesn't feel like I'm running to keep up with him. The
streets are packed with people, all seemingly walking in the same
direction as if by instinct. It feels both different and the same
being with Kareem again. Or this version of Kareem. This new
Kareem talks about his feelings with his dad yet still remembers
my favorite ice cream combo. I want to tell him about all the
films and shows I've watched over the last four months. But it's
not like he's just coming back from a long vacation. We broke up.
Don't know if those convos are allowed anymore. Is it possible
for us to be friends again? Is that what I really want?

We make our way through midtown to Union Square,
heading deep into the Village, moving closer to downtown.
Closer to . . . the bridge.

"How much longer do you think the power's gonna be out
for?" I ask, not bothering to hide the panic in my voice. "Like, it
can't be all night, right?"

He shrugs, mind elsewhere. "Maybe."

I start to ask what's wrong, but that ain't my place. Or at least I don't think it is.

"Kareem, I –"

My phone buzzes. An unknown number. Kareem looks over and brightens.

"Oh shit, that's Twig," he says and presses speaker. "What's up!"

"Yo, fam! Where you at?"

"Still in the city, but making moves," he says, checking the time. "What's good?"

"Nothing. That's what's good. I'm trying to throw the party of the summer and everything's working against me. Just get your ass here with quickness. Peace!"

Click.

"Okay. He ain't much for talking." I laugh.

"That's Twig for you," he says, before turning his head. "Hey, you hear that?"

Music. A deep bass from nearby.

He throws me a sly grin and nods ahead. "Yo, let's check out the park for a second."

I don't argue. The more time we waste on detours, the more chances of the power turning back on before it's too late.

We pass under the large white arch at the entrance of Washington Square Park. When the power is on, this thing is lit up bright white, reminds me of that big famous arch in Paris we learned about in European History. It leads to a massive fountain in the middle of the park, surrounded by benches and patches of grass. This is where all the New York University students and Village folk hang out. Even with the blackout, the place is packed, bands playing music, chess games in the dark, teens skateboarding.

"Ew! I can't believe people are swimming in that nasty-ass fountain," I say, watching a white woman sit neck deep in the murky pool.

"You blame them? It's mad hot out here," he says, laughing. "Hey, wasn't NYU your first choice?"

I rub my hands against my dress. "Um, yeah."

Back when I wanted to stay in the city.

Back when I wanted to still be close to him.

Back when my life and all the things I wanted included him.

We find the source of the music: a portable speaker playing Bob Marley's "Is This Love." A small crowd of hipsters dance and sing along.

"Ohhhh, okay! I knew I recognized this tune! It's your people's music!"

I roll my eyes. "Of course the white kids with dreads smoking weed on a college campus would be playing Bob Marley."

"Come now," he teases in a fake Jamaican accent while two-stepping, waving me on. "You trying to bust a whine?"

"Boy, quit playing," I laugh.

He takes my hand and spins me around. "One dance won't hurt."

I slip right into his arms and even though this isn't exactly a slow song, we sway slow, to our own rhythm. My arms instinctively find their way up his shoulders. His skin is sweaty and hot, his hands grip my waist . . . my neck is burning, the sky is spinning and I'm focusing on his feet because if I look up into his eyes I know, just know, I'll kiss him. His lips graze my forehead, and my whole body shivers.

Girl, what you doing!

I jump back five feet.

"You okay?" he asks, frowning, as if he's confused by his empty hands.

"Yeah, I'm good," I squeak, searching for a distraction. Another speaker is playing a hip-hop beat on the opposite side of the fountain. A group of kids sets off a rap cypher, the crowd bobbing their heads. Kareem bobs along with them.

"Aye, whose beat is this?" he asks a guy near the speaker. "Shit is fire!"

As they chat, the crowd thickens and I struggle to take a deep breath, tugging on his shirt. Too many people. Waaaaay too many people.

"Um, we should get going."

"Hold up one second," he says, turning to me. "Lemme see your phone again?"

I hand him my phone, and he opens up Google, pulling up a weird music page, then grabs the aux cord from the speaker.

"Aight. Let's see how y'all rock to this!"

Kareem puts on a new beat and the cypher continues, the crowd rocking along, asking him about his music. The beat is smooth, chill, something that anyone could rap over but that also makes everyone vibe to it.

"Thanks, man," he says to the guy manning the speaker as they wrap up. "Yo, hit me up anytime!"

We walk off, heading for the exit, Kareem cheesing.

"That . . . was so dope, Kareem," I squeal. "You made that beat on your phone?"

"Yeah," he says, beaming. "I think they gonna hit me up for more beats. Maybe DJ a party."

"I didn't know you were trying to make . . . like a career out of this."

"Don't see how, it's all I talked about."

"Yeah but . . . I didn't think you were serious."

Kareem smile fades instantly. "Well, yeah. I was. My dad even convinced me to switch my major to audio engineering."

So that's how he was able to apply for the internship. He switched majors. And I guess that would explain why he was so into going to all those parties. He really has always been obsessed with music.

He tips his chin at a building ahead of us. "Aye yo, what made you change your mind about NYU?"

Glancing up at the NYU Library, I cook up a quick lie. "And waste all my money to go to school blocks from my mother's house? No thanks!"

"Yeah," he sighs. "But going to any college cost money, even the local ones. That's why I need that Apollo gig. And all the DJ gigs I can get."

Local ones? So he must be going to St. John's with Imani. She's been bragging all over school how she got a full scholarship. He wants the internship so he can go to college with her . . . instead of me. He's being all nice and flirty so he can trick me into dropping out of the position.

Just like my cousin said, "He's a pretty boy. You can't trust those types."

"Why'd we come this way?" I snap, crossing my arms. "We should've stayed on Broadway."

He shrugs. "I don't know. Thought a quick drive-by would help change your mind. Not be in such a rush to run away."

I fake a laugh. "Ha! I'm not running away."

He cocks his lips to the side. "Yo, you don't think I know you, but I do know you, Tammi. You're only trying to leave early because of what happened with us."

He's up to something.

A lump rises up to my throat, skin prickling. It's a bull's-eye hit I wasn't expecting.

"That's not true. Clark Atlanta was always on the list of colleges I wanted us to go to. I even filled out an application for you!"

He laughs. "Let me ask you something – you ever consider how I was gonna pay for all those schools you picked out for us? You have your parents to take out loans and shit. What about me? You know my folks can't afford to send me anywhere."

My mouth drops to defend myself, but I come up empty. I never once thought about the logistics of how we'd go school together. I was just so focused on getting there.

He shakes his head. "You wanted to go to NYU. That was your dream. I knew I couldn't afford NYU, but I still thought we'd be here, in New York . . . together."

"Well, things change!" I reply. "Clearly."

"Not everything has to," he says.

I throw up my hands. "Why, Kareem? Why after months of silence, why do you have so much to say now? All this time you could've talked to me and now you coming out your neck."

He closes the distance between us, grabbing both of my hands.

"You know me," he says. "I ain't good with words and shit. That was your job! But I'm talking now. Is it too late?"

He leans down, resting his forehead on mine. I hold my breath as a voice inside me says, He's right, I do know him! I know him more than I know myself.

"Is it too late?" he asks again, inching toward my lips, and the world starts spinning faster.

"Kareem," I gasp, just as the phone rings in my bag, bringing me back to reality.

"It's, um, my mom."

Kareem straightens as I put the phone on speaker. "Hey, baby. You guys okay? I have Kareem's mom on the line too."

"Hey, Tammi!" Mrs. Murphy says. "How y'all doing?"

"Fine," we answer in unison.

"Everything good?" Kareem asks.

"Kareem, don't you remember? G-Ma moved to a home up on the Upper West Side on Wednesday. To be with her friend, Pearl."

Kareem hits his forehead. "Shit. I forgot!"

"Upper West Side? We were just there!"

"I know, but don't worry," Mom says. "My friend's daughter Nella is there visiting her grandpa and says she's doing fine. Helping to keep others calm."

I click off with Mom as Kareem stares in the direction we came from.

"Should we go back?" I ask.

He sighs. "Nah, we're almost to the bridge. And your phone's at thirty-five percent. We just need to get to Brooklyn."

I nod. "Um, okay."

The music grows faint as we head down West Fourth Street. I always imagined us taking long walks around here, but as college students. Now . . . I don't know what I want anymore. All I know is that I miss him, and even though it has to, deep down, I don't want this day to ever end.

Just as we turn back on Broadway, a red double-decker bus dips in and out of traffic and I catch a quick glimpse of the driver.

"Hey!" I shout, running into the street after it, waving frantically. But the bus was already through the next light, making its way to Chinatown.

Kareem catches up to me. "Yoooo! Was that your –"

"I think so." I laugh in disbelief.

"Damn! We could've got a ride! Well, at least to the bridge."

This day has been a mess from start to finish.

"Let's keep going, I guess." I sigh, fanning my neck.

We walk in silence again before Kareem snickers. "Yo, if I didn't say it before, good looking out back there with old boy in Times Square." He laughs, bumping my shoulder. "Definitely wouldn't have gotten the job after beating the life out of that chump."

We catch eyes, nervously blinking away. Looks like we both need that job more than we'd like to admit. The blackout brought us back together – will the Apollo internship rip us apart?

NO SLEEP TILL BROOKLYN

Angie Thomas

Double-decker bus, downtown New York City, 9:07 p.m.
Let's start with the facts:

There are twelve hundred miles between Jackson, Mississippi, and New York City.

It takes two flights and a mad dash through the Atlanta airport to get to New York City.

The Atlanta airport is too damn big to make any kinda "mad dash" through.

There are 2.9 million people in the entire state of Mississippi.

There are 8.3 million people in New York City alone.

Yet even in a blackout, New York doesn't feel big enough when you're sitting next to your boyfriend while four seats away from your crush.

The double-decker tour bus creeps down some busy Manhattan street, past a park with a stone archway entrance. According to our bus driver, Mr. Wright, it's Washington Square Park. If it weren't for that, this would look like any other Manhattan street to me – skyscrapers towering above, packed sidewalks, and traffic-jammed streets.

My first thought when we arrived in New York? Everything's cramped as hell.

Second thought? Everybody stays busy.

The blackout hasn't even stopped that. My whole class was on this bus when the lights went out. Picture it, twelve rising juniors plus a first-year teacher on a class trip from Mississippi. Scratch that – twelve *Black* rising juniors from an "inner-city school" (does anybody say "outer city"?) with their twenty-something-year-old white woman teacher when a blackout hits the Big Apple.

Fact: New Yorkers don't call it "the Big Apple," just like Atlanta folks don't call it "Hotlanta." A couple of us Mississippi folks do call it "Da Sip," though.

We all freaked when the power first went out. We hit up social media and discovered that it was a city-wide power outage. Then our phones blew up as our families back home checked on us. My daddy, a southern Black man through and through, was like, "See? I don't trust that New York mess. I knew we shouldn't have let you go up there."

Daddy has an *interesting* relationship with New York. He and Momma visited once back in 2003 to come see Daddy's younger brother, Graham, and there was a major blackout back then. Kinda ironic that I'm in one now. 'Til this day, Daddy will tell you all about how he and Momma were sightseeing on the Brooklyn Bridge and had to walk back to their hotel in Manhattan because of the blackout. Momma was pregnant with me, too. Had just found out a week before. Daddy claims his feet are still calloused from the journey.

"That's the last city that ever needs to be without lights," he always says. "I ain't scared of much, but you couldn't pay me to be in New York during a blackout again."

New York *is* kinda creepy with all the lights out. Headlights and brake lights glow for miles and miles, the brightest things around. People shine the flashlights on their phones as they navigate the sidewalks. I think the weirdest part of all of this is that shit don't stop. Back home, a power outage is a good excuse to sit outside and do nothing, especially during a heat wave like today. Here, everybody's finding a way to keep it moving and keep it mostly calm.

Mrs. Tucker ain't one of them. Poor woman is on the verge of a breakdown. She goes over the class roll for the fifty-millionth time, like somehow one of us snuck off this bus.

"Rashad?" she calls out.

"Present," he says, from the first row.

"Jazmyn."

"Here," my bestie says behind me.

"Kayla?"

"Here," I say.

"Tre'Shawn?"

"Here," my boyfriend says beside me. He gives me a smirk, probably thinking, *how long before this lady loses her mind.* When she does, it'll fill in one more spot on the Karen Bingo we got in the class group chat for every time Mrs. Tucker does something Karenish. Take yesterday morning, for example. We had arrived at LaGuardia and were filing onto the shuttle bus to go to the hotel when Mrs. Tucker asked our Latinx driver what country he was from.

"Jersey," he said.

"No, where are you *from-from*?" she asked, in the kinda tone you use on a kindergartner. She's lucky that man didn't cuss her out.

Back to Tre'Shawn. I hate that he looks so cute when he smirks. His dimples appear – it doesn't take much for them to show – and his light brown eyes get this twinkle in them that melt me. I'm supposed to be mad at him, dammit. So I roll my eyes and stare ahead.

He groans. "Kay, c'mon. You still upset that I–"

"Micah," Mrs. Tucker calls out louder than usual. That's her way of telling Tre'Shawn to be quiet while she takes roll. She really does act like we're preschoolers.

"Present," Micah says with an easy smile a couple of rows ahead of us. Even in the blackout, he's fine. Black boys with dark skin tend to look majestic in the moonlight. He lounges in a seat to himself, his long legs stretched across it and his back to the bustle of New York as if he doesn't wanna gawk at people like the rest of us. But I think he's sitting that way so he can see me.

You see, he sent me a text a few hours ago. Seven words that could shake everything up:

Do I have a shot, lil momma?

I've left it on read since I saw it.

Because I don't know.

Which kinda makes me a shitty girlfriend.

Who shouldn't be mad at Tre'Shawn.

Because ditching your girlfriend to hang with your homies and lying about it isn't as big of a deal as talking to somebody else.

And flirting with somebody else.

And purposely finding ways to spend time with somebody else.

Like going to study hall when you know he'll be there.

Or deciding to do a story in the school paper about the track team just because it means you'll have to interview him.

Then letting him take you home after school one day.

And laughing and talking and getting so caught up that when he leans over the gears and tries to kiss you.

You almost let him.

But you don't. I didn't.

I just *almost* did.

Which is still bad.

Mrs. Tucker finishes the roll – yes, everybody is exactly where they were when she checked forty-five minutes ago – and heads to the lower level.

"Behave, everyone," she says in a singsong voice. "I'm going to check with the driver and see why we're not moving anymore."

Um, maybe because the traffic lights are out, and cars were already bumper to bumper before that? We're the only ones left on the bus. All the other tourists hopped off a while ago and decided to walk. Never happening with Mrs. Tucker.

She disappears down the steps, and the second she's gone, we all bust out laughing.

"Ay, five dollars say she ask the driver if she can speak to his manager," Rashad says.

"Pshhhhiiiid, fool, she probably already did," says Jaysean, not to be confused with Tre'Shawn. First day of school, Mrs. Tucker asked if they were twin brothers even though they don't look alike. They just have similar first names and the same last name.

"No, ma'am," Jaysean told her. "Our ancestors were probably owned by the same slave master, though."

The look on that woman's face was priceless.

Aja leans over the railing of the bus. "Why the hell these people still going into restaurants? Don't they know it's a blackout?"

"They still gotta eat, Aja, dang," I say. We've been real touristy, I gotta admit. We say "they" and "them" a lot 'cause even though we're all humans, New Yorkers may as well be aliens compared to us. It's fascinating to watch them.

Not like they don't do us the same way. This morning we grabbed breakfast at the hotel restaurant, and the waitress was like, "Where are you guys from?"

"Mississippi," we all said.

"Oh my God!" She acted like we said Mars. "Your accents!"

I honestly didn't notice that I had one until I started talking in New York. Now I realize that my words ooze out like maple syrup, a foreign sound to them. They spit theirs out fast, like holding them too long will burn their tongues. A southerner just has to try to catch up.

My uncle Graham claims he was quiet when he first moved to New York because he was ashamed of his accent. He likes to tell people he "ran from Mississippi like Flo Jo with a fire on her behind" and never looked back. He and his husband, Jean Claude, live in Brooklyn with their daughter, Lana, and son, Langston. I was hoping to go to Brooklyn to visit them somehow, but I doubt I can get away from Mrs. Tucker for a couple of hours.

Jaysean leans over the rail of the tour bus. We're inching along, at the end of the park. Washington Square Park, I think that's what it is. "I could fuck up some pizza right now," Jaysean says.

"Forget pizza, I'm tryna holla," says Rashad. He leans over the railing and yells out, "Ay, shawty! What that mouth do?"

Ewww! He would say some nasty mess like that.

"Man, have some manners!" says Micah. "Act like you been somewhere before."

"You know damn well that fool ain't been nowhere," Tre'Shawn says, and he and Micah share a laugh. Tre'Shawn doesn't know that in some ways they've been sharing parts of me, too.

Tre'Shawn looks at me, a boyish smile playing at his lips. "I'm just lucky I ain't gotta holla at nobody. I got everything I need right here."

He leans over to kiss me, and I feel Micah watching.

I pull back, but not 'cause of Micah. I don't think.

Tre'Shawn sighs. "Dang, Kayla. You won't let this go, huh? It's been almost a week."

"You lied to me, Tre."

"Yep! On period," Jazmyn says behind us.

Tre'Shawn glares back at her. "Mind your business, damn!" He looks at me. "I told you I'm sorry. Is it really that big of a deal?"

"It must've been for you to lie about it," I say. "All you had to do was tell me you were hanging with your boys. Why say you were sick just to skip being with me?"

It aches my throat to even say that. Now, let me be clear: I am not a clingy girlfriend. And even if I was, that doesn't make it cool to lie.

Tre'Shawn is quiet at first. The bus picks up a little speed and makes a turn, causing a car near us to honk. That's the soundtrack of New York City – honking horns. I've heard more of them in two days here than I've heard my whole life back home. Our driver, Mr. Wright, fusses from the main level of the bus, spitting out cuss-words in his thick Jamaican accent. Earlier, Mrs. Tucker asked him where he was from, too.

"Earth," he said. "Still debating if I'm staying, though."

The class group chat agreed – he's our favorite bus driver so far.

After a moment, Tre'Shawn sighs. "I guess I didn't wanna upset you, Kayla. You know I don't like to let you down. And if we keeping it one hunnid? That show you wanted us to binge-watch looked corny as shit."

"For your information, I pick out good shows."

"The same way you pick out good football teams?" he says.

"Um, as a Falcons fan, you cannot *ever* talk about other teams being bad," I say. "Y'all were up twenty-eight to three and *still* lost the Super Bowl to the Patriots."

He winces. "You had to go there, huh?"

"You asked for it by throwing shade at my Saints," I say. "Don't be mad because you're probably the only Falcons fan in the entire state of Mississippi."

Tre pretends to cough. "The Ain'ts" he says, and coughs again.

I examine his hand. "That's a nice Super Bowl ring you've – ah, nope. Not one."

Tre snatches his hand away, and I bust out laughing. Back home, football is religion, and the Saints are . . . well, the patron saints. I was practically born in black and gold. The first outfit my daddy put on me was a Saints jersey. (The second one was a Jackson State University T-shirt because JSU is a sub-religion in our house, followed closely by Delta Sigma Theta sorority and Omega Psi Phi fraternity.)

We watch every Saints game as a family – me, Momma, Daddy, my big sister, Ciara, and my big brother, Junior – and we often make the three-hour drive to NOLA to our beloved Superdome. It's a miracle Tre'Shawn and I have lasted this long with him being a fan of the Falcons. My family calls them the Failcons. One time the Saints were playing the Falcons, and Daddy and Junior forbid Tre from coming in the house. Said he'd have to watch from the porch. Momma let him in but made him sit on the other side of the den. At least she compromised.

Tre cups my cheek. "Awful football choices aside, I love you," he says. "Hanging with my boys was fun, but at the end of the day I would much rather been with you, watching that corny show."

"Or even a Saints game?" I ask.

Tre frowns. "I guess. But I'd definitely root against them."

"You're a sad, sad man."

"Whatever, Kay," he says, with a laugh. "Can you forgive me?"

Out the corner of my eye, I see Micah watching us. The fact that I care that he's watching gives me no right to be mad at Tre'Shawn.

"Yeah. I forgive you."

I let him kiss me this time. It's comforting and familiar. I could kiss a hundred people with my eyes closed, and I could easily pick out Tre'Shawn's lips from the rest. He's been my first everything – first kiss in fourth grade, first boyfriend in eighth, first love, first person I had sex with. We've been a couple for so long that people at school practically combine our names. Tre-N-Kay. Everyone expects us to be together forever. What do I look like, not living up to their expectations?

That's who I am. Kayla Simmons, expectations meeter. Besides, I love Tre. I could honestly see myself with him for the rest of my life.

But every now and then there's this little voice in my head that wonders if that's because he's the only person I've ever been with. It's kinda like jeans. I know that sounds weird, but when you get that one pair that just goes right with everything, it's hard to let them go. That one pair is usually as comfortable as sweatpants, too, and they're perfect on those frustrating days where nothing else fits right. That's Tre'Shawn for me.

Wait, am I really comparing my boyfriend to a pair of jeans?

I ignore all of that and kiss Tre' some more. I love the taste of his lips, sweet and sticky 'cause of the cotton candy we shared earlier in Times Square before we hopped on the tour bus. His hand travels under my T-shirt, fingers gently grazing my back. That his go-to move. He likes the way it gives me goose bumps.

"Hey, hey, hey! No, no, no!" Mrs. Tucker bounds down the aisle. She pulls me back from Tre'Shawn. I almost ask her what gives her the right to touch me.

"No hooking up, please!" she says, sounding real strained. I mean, the Karen is all up in her voice. "Kayla, sit with Jazmyn. Tre'Shawn, you sit with Micah."

Oh, shit.

No.

New York City just got a whole lot smaller.

"This is SoHo," Mr. Wright, our driver, says, "where they'll charge you a salary for a glass of water and call it gourmet."

Everybody laughs, even Mrs. On-the-Edge Tucker. We've finally gotten away from Washington Square Park. Mr. Wright has been cussing other drivers out left and right so he can maneuver the streets and continue our tour of the city. Either Mrs. Tucker went Karenator on him, aka the final form of Karen, or he's dedicated to his job. I doubt that man is shook by her, so he's probably dedicated to his job.

SoHo seems to be my kinda place. There are upscale boutiques everywhere that sell clothes I may never be able to afford. A girl can look, though. The architecture of the neighborhood screams artsy. In fact, the word *artsy* was probably made just to describe SoHo. This is the one neighborhood Momma still talks about to this day. She said it was her favorite place to people watch when she and Daddy visited.

Now here I am, watching people sit at tables outside of restaurants and have candlelit dinners. This one couple has their chairs together close and they cuddle up to look at a phone, the light of it illuminating their faces. It's too cute not to stare.

I bet neither one of them ever compared the other one to jeans or caught feelings for someone else.

I stretch my neck to try to catch a glance at Tre and Micah for the millionth time. Mrs. Tucker's new seating arrangements took Rashad from the front row and put him directly in front of me. Mrs. Tucker's in his old seat now so she can "have a good view of all of us." But wide-shouldered Rashad is making it hard for me to see my boyfriend and my –

My nothing-but-something. That's what Micah is.

"Girl, you okay?" Jazmyn asks beside me.

Not in the least bit. "Yeah. I'm good."

"Leave it to Tuckaren to kill somebody's vibe," she says. She uses a pen to scratch a hard-to-reach spot under her bun.

She says something else, but I miss it because Micah and Tre'Shawn are laughing up front. I know both of their laughs well enough to recognize them without seeing them. Tre does this kinda, *ki-ki* laugh that literally sounds like he's saying "ki-ki." Micah's laughs come straight from his gut and sound like somebody's granddaddy who used to smoke.

Fact: Being fine does not mean you automatically have a nice laugh.

Listening to them laugh makes my brain do that annoying thing where it immediately thinks the worst. My therapist says it's part of my anxiety – expect bad stuff as opposed to good things so I won't be hurt. Anxiety plays the most frustrating mind games. My therapist gave me some exercises to try to combat it, but not a single method is working right now. Instead I'm wondering if Micah and Tre'Shawn are laughing about me. I'm one of the main things they have in common, right? It would make sense.

Micah's probably like, *Yo, did she freak out the first time you tried to kiss her, too?*

And Tre goes, *Nah, bruh, but we were in like fourth grade. Didn't know what the hell we were doing anyway. She was scared as hell that she got pregnant 'cause our tongues touched.*

And that would lead to them laughing like they are right now.

"Kay!" Jazmyn says my name like it's her tenth time calling me. "Dang, girl. What's wrong with you, for real?"

I seriously have to get out of my own head. "Sorry. What's up?"

"I said, are you and Tre'Shawn good?"

"For now, yeah."

"For now?" Jazymn says. "Is he on some fuck boy shit?"

I roll my eyes. "Jazzy. Tre'Shawn is not a fuck boy."

"He lied so he could hang out with those idiots he calls friends. Sounds like one to me."

I shake my head at her. I've gotta admit, every single person on earth needs a Jazzy in their life. She's been my best friend since before I knew what a friend was. Our parents were soros and frat brothers, and they tailgated at every JSU football game together. Jazzy's parents filed for divorce a few months ago, so that's not happening anymore. She's quick to stick up for me. Probably too quick at times. But hey, I go just as hard for her, too. You mess with one of us, you mess with both of us. And that's on that.

When it comes to Tre'Shawn, she's not a fan at all. I don't honestly get it. Pretty much everybody loves Tre'. But ever since our elementary school days, Jazzy will take one look at Tre'Shawn, roll her eyes, and hiss, "Ooooh, I can't stand him!"

In other words, this ain't new.

"He wasn't being a fuck boy," I tell her. "He just didn't wanna binge-watch my shows."

"That's a sorry reason to lie, Kay," she says. "I don't be wanting to watch your corny shows either, but at least I tell you to your face."

"Excuse you?"

"Kayla," she says, tilting her head. Her tone makes it seem like this is a come-to-Jesus meeting. "Don't nobody wanna watch *Gilmore Girls* reruns but you. Own that."

"Whatever. It's better than watching the same episodes of *Supernatural* over and over like *some* people."

"That is one of the greatest shows to ever exist, and you will deal," she says.

"Mmmhmmm, sure," I say, as my phone vibrates in my lap. It's my family. Again. Because I'm the baby of the Simmons gang, you'd think that my parents would've been a bit more chill with me. They managed to get two other kids to adulthood in one piece each, you know? Maybe they could loosen the reins a bit. Never. In fact, instead of having two parents, I kinda have four with my brother and sister. The family group chat has been popping since the blackout. This time, it's my sister, Ciara. It's around nine a.m. in Tokyo, where she's doing a semester.

Kay-Kay, y'all still stuck on the bus?

Before I can even reply, my brother, Junior, butts in.

Get out and walk, sis.

Then he adds, You and Tre better not be fooling around in the dark.

Oh my God. I quickly type out, I'm not walking. I don't know where to go. And don't worry about us.

I barely put my phone down when it dings again. This time, it's Daddy.

What the hell is that supposed to mean?

I can't with them right now. I can't.

Luckily, Momma comes to the rescue.

I'm sure Mrs. Tucker is keeping a close eye on them, Freddie. That woman could work for the Secret Service, as thorough as she is.

Then Daddy goes, I still don't trust that New York mess. This could be more than just a little blackout. Something more serious.

It wasn't in 2003, Momma adds.

Luckily, Daddy writes. Besides, you were the one who panicked the most back then.

Ooop, Ciara writes.

I send the two eyes emoji.

Momma sends back the side-eye one.

Kay-Kay, keep trying your Uncle Graham, Daddy writes. If you can't get him, find the US Embassy. Tell them your grandaddy was a Vietnam vet. They'll help you out.

Is this man serious?

Ciara writes back, Daddy, there's no need for a US embassy in New York. It's part of the United States.

Daddy goes, Could've fooled me! Whole different country from here!

Here comes Junior.

That's not necessarily a bad thing . . .

Then Daddy says, Boy, you're Mississippi born and bred. Don't act brand-new 'cause you're in Dallas.

Momma says, Now that's a whole different country. Texas is like its own continent.

Ciara says, It's bigger than some countries too.

Hold up. How did this become a geography lesson all of a sudden? I sigh and type, Gotta save my battery. Putting my phone away. Will keep y'all posted. Love you!

I stick my phone in my backpack and peek up ahead again. Tre'Shawn and Micah are having a real animated conversation. Micah's hands never stay still as he talks, and Tre tends to nod a lot. In some universe, they would be best friends. They like the same video games, the same music, the same sports. The same girl.

Sometimes I wonder if that's really why I caught feelings for Micah, because he's so similar to what I already know. Same brand of jeans but a different style. I've quickly realized though there's not always logic with feelings. Logic is a brain thing, and the heart has a mind of its own. It doesn't need the brain, no matter how much I wish it did.

"Okay, what's up?" Jazmyn says.

I look at her. "Huh?"

"Why are you on the verge of freaking out over Tre being up there?"

"I'm not freaking –"

"Kay, you can't see your face, but I can," she says. "You're almost breaking a sweat, and don't tell me it's 'cause of this 'heat wave' either. This is cool compared to at home."

Very true. New Yorkers love to complain about the heat and

humidity here, and I'm still trying to figure out what humidity they're talking about. Mississippi is a gigantic sauna for most of the year. This is nothing.

I rub the back of my neck. Jazzy's gonna bug me 'til I spill. I haven't told anybody about me and Micah. Not that there's a me and Micah. But the stuff going on between us, *if* there's something going on between us – see? I don't even know where to begin.

So I don't. I pull up the text message and hand Jazzy my phone.

It lights up her face in the dark, and her eyes get wide. "Holy sh– Kay." She looks at me. "This is from –"

I nod. "Yep."

"Have y'all been –?"

"We've nothing," I say. "Well, we hung out a few times. That's it."

"When? You didn't tell me!"

I should've known that was coming. "It wasn't a big deal, Jazzy."

"Um, it was to someone." She holds my phone up.

I sigh through my nose. "Apparently."

"You feel the same way?"

I shrug.

"Damn," she says, and hands me my phone. "This is a lot, Kay."

"I know. And now–" I nod at my boyfriend sitting with my crush.

"No wonder you're freaking out."

"Right." I close my eyes. My head throbs from all the drama. "What should I do, Jazzy?"

I've wanted to ask somebody that for months now, but I never knew who I could ask. Jazmyn's usually my first choice, but her parents' divorce is enough for her to deal with. My second option is Ciara, but I didn't wanna dump this on her. It seems minor compared with all she's dealing with while being Black in Japan. There's no third or fourth option who won't tell my business all over the school. My mom? She'd be like, *Give it to God, baby.* I doubt that God cares about high school love triangles when there are famines and disease all over the world.

Jazmyn scratches her hair with her pen again. "The answer is obvious, Kay. Drop Tre'Shawn and get with that fine-ass Micah."

I almost choke. "What?"

"You heard me. You should've *been* dropped that fool. I can name a thousand legitimate reasons why y'all shouldn't be together."

"Jazzy, I'm not trying to hear your anti-Tre'Shawn campaign. I need a non-biased opinion, please."

"Um, I said all of my reasons are legitimate. Do you wanna hear them or not?"

I sigh and turn toward her, my back to the hustle and bustle below. "Fine. List ten of them. Only ten," I say, with a warning eye. "I don't wanna hear this all night."

"All right, fine, let's see. Number one: he thinks he's all that."

"He does not!"

"Ha! Girl, yes he does," she says. "He walks around school like he's God's gift to the human race. He cute, but he ain't fine-fine."

"That's a matter of opinion," I say. "What else?"

"His laugh is reason enough," Jazzy says. "Sounds like he's strangling on water and trying to clear his throat."

Okay, that *is* a pretty accurate description. "I think it's a cute laugh."

"You're brainwashed; of course you do. Three, his jokes are corny. Okay yeah, sometimes they make me laugh but dang, boy. Get better material."

I laugh. "Quit hating."

"All facts, boo. No hate. Four, when he smiles, his eyes light up and make him look like a total goofball," she says. "Five, he cannot dance. He has that one lil move that he does over and over again but for some silly reason, he thinks he's got skills.

"Six, he wears the same cologne all the time. I'm always like damn, switch it up, my dude. Nope, he only wears Ralph Lauren Polo. Every time I smell it, I think of him now. Seven, he licks his lips a lot, especially when he's thinking hard. Eight, his hands are way too soft. Nine, that little fuzz above his lip. Grow it or cut it, please. Ten, speaking of lips, his are way too plump in the first place. And bam, there you go. Ten reasons," she says.

"Wow," I say, as I look at her. "You noticed all of that?"

"Yeah." Jazmyn shrugs. "How can I not?"

How can *I* not?

Half the stuff Jazmyn just said, I haven't paid much attention to. Here I am, his girlfriend, and I hadn't realized he only has one dance move or that he licks his lips a lot. The cologne thing I knew. He wears Ralph Lauren because I love it so much.

But it's not really bothering me that *I* didn't notice all of these small details. It's the fact that my best friend did.

It makes me think of something my mom once said. She and Daddy first met at Jackson State their freshman year. Daddy was a drum major, and Momma said he didn't walk around campus, he *strutted*, as if he knew he was "all that and a bag of chips."

"Lord, I couldn't stand that man," she said. "Every small thing about Freddie Simmons irked me with a passion. But one day, I realized something. All those small things irked me mostly because I was mad at myself for being attracted to them. I had strong feelings for that man, all right, just not in the way I thought. They're not lying when they say there's a thin line between love and hate."

I stare at Jazmyn. For years, I couldn't explain her disdain for Tre'Shawn, but now it's like I finally see a part of her that she's hidden. Or maybe it was there all along, and I didn't wanna see it.

"We're girls, right?" I say.

"You even gotta ask that? Of course we are."

"And you'll be completely honest with me, right?"

"Absolutely," Jazzy says.

I bite my lip. "Do you . . . do you secretly *like* Tre'Shawn?"

Her eyes widen. "What – Kay –"

"Hold up, what you say?" Tre'Shawn snaps up ahead. He's out of his seat and towering over Micah. Micah looks ready to rise, but Mrs. Tucker quickly scrambles over.

She pulls my boyfriend away. "No fighting!" she says. "New seating arrangement! Kayla, come sit here with Micah. Tre'Shawn, you sit with Jazmyn."

Shit.

My night keeps getting worse.

"What did you say to him?"

"I told you, Kayla. I didn't say much," Micah claims.

"Okay, but *what* did you say?"

The bus creeps through Chinatown. Mr. Wright said it's home to one of the best ice cream shops in the city.

I miss the days when all it took was an ice cream cone to fix everything. There's not enough ice cream in the world for all I'm dealing with.

I glance back. The moonlight just barely reveals Tre'Shawn with his jaw set hard and his eyes in our direction. Jazmyn sits straight as a board at the very end of the seat they share, as far as possible from my boyfriend as she can be.

She's sent me a bunch of texts. I haven't read any of them yet.

Micah watches Chinatown pass by. "It's dope how there are all these different pockets in the city that are so unique. Which neighborhood do you think you'd live in?"

"Stop trying to change the subject and answer my question,"

I say. "What did you tell Tre'Shawn?"

Micah shrugs. Nothing ever seems to bother him. As someone diagnosed with anxiety, I envy it, even admire it. At the moment it's frustrating as hell.

"I said the truth, Kay," he says.

My heart pounds. "Which is?"

"That it was really shitty of him to lie to you just to hang with his friends, and that he better watch out or someone else may scoop you up."

Holy – "You didn't. Micah, you didn't."

He shrugs again. "I keep it real. Didn't you say that's one reason you like me? Even highlighted it in your piece in the school paper."

I did. It was one of the main reasons Micah's track team-mates said they made him captain – he's honest to a fault and he expects honesty right back. The guy you can trust with just about anything. I once wondered if hearts were included.

"It doesn't matter," I tell him and myself. "It wasn't your place to say that."

"I have no problem speaking up for someone I care about," Micah says.

I glance away. It's hard to look at Micah when he talks like that. Best way I can describe it is like staring into the sun. You know it's not good for you, but part of you wants to stare because of the warmth it gives.

"It still wasn't your place to say that," I mumble. "Now he's mad."

"Let him be. You were mad when he lied and ghosted you."

"I forgave him earlier," I say.

"Did it take lying to yourself to do that?"

"What do I have to lie to myself about?"

"You tell me," Micah says.

I shake my head, 'cause that's easier to do than respond. "Just stop, Micah."

"Fine," he says. He turns to watch the streets below.

Micah first transferred to our school last year, right after Christmas. Until then, I didn't know it was possible for someone to turn my life upside down with so little effort. He'd catch my eye in the hall, and my whole face would get warm. He'd scoot his desk near mine when our teacher put us in a group together, and I'd secretly hope that our arms might brush or our feet might touch. After every encounter, I'd beat myself up for having those feelings.

Sitting so close to him now, I've got butterflies in my stomach. I wish they'd drop dead.

Out of nowhere, Micah goes, "You notice how in New York, people can be here and not be here?"

I look at him. "What?"

"Like over there." He nods at this couple who are clearly tourists. They point out the buildings, even in the dark. "They're here-here. Noticing everything around them. But then you got somebody like that dude." He points at this guy whose eyes are completely on his phone as he walks. "Chinatown is just a sidewalk to him. He knows it so well, he doesn't even have to look where he's going."

"Probably a native New Yorker," I say.

"Probably. But even if I was from here, I'd rather be like them." He points out the couple again. "In awe of all the things instead of not appreciating them because they've always been there."

He looks at me as he says it.

"What are you trying to get at?"

He leans a little closer to me. "Who said I'm trying to get at anything?"

Fact: anytime Micah gets close to me, I get goose bumps, as if my skin comes alive at the thought of him touching it. Anticipation can be torture if you let it.

I scoot away and glance back. Tre'Shawn watches, but I can't read his face in the dark, which is worse.

"I didn't mean to piss him off," Micah claims.

I look at him again. "Oh really?"

"Promise. I never said *I* was trying to scoop you up. Homie got mad at the idea of me saying *somebody* might."

"Because you don't say that to another person about their girlfriend, Micah."

"Even though it's true?" he asks. "He's damn lucky to have you, baby girl."

Logic says that having a girlfriend who purposely tries to hang out with another boy isn't exactly luck. "That's sweet of you to say, but you don't really know me, Micah."

"Then let me get to know you." He turns all the way toward

me. "Let's play twenty questions."

"What?"

"Twenty questions. We gotta do something to pass time."

"Micah, stop trying to –"

"Get to know you a little more without any ulterior motives?" he asks. "No funny business. Promise. Like I said, it's just a game to pass time."

We *are* moving slow again – I could probably walk faster than this bus is going. It wouldn't hurt to do something to keep me from getting worked up. This could easily become the tour bus ride from anxiety hell any moment.

"Fine," I say. "I start first though."

"Of course. Shoot."

"All right. What's your biggest fear?" I ask.

"Dang. Trying to make a dude vulnerable from jump," he says. "Drowning. I fell into a pool when I was two. Still remember it in flashes. I've hated water ever since. What's yours?"

"Can't come up with an original question? Wow," I tease, and he rolls his eyes. "Losing everyone I love is my biggest fear. I cried like a baby when my sister moved overseas and my brother went to Dallas. Stupid, because they're still alive. But it hit that fear, I guess."

Micah nods slowly. "I can get that. I'd probably feel some kinda way if I had siblings and they moved away."

"I forgot you're an only child."

"Proudly," he says. "We catch a lot of flak but we're dope as hell. Just don't like to share much."

"As the baby of my family, I was spoiled and didn't like to share either, so I get it. Okay, next question: cat or dog person?"

"Dogs all day. Cats are demons."

I gasp. "What? How dare you!"

Micah puts his hands up. "Hey, don't shoot the messenger, all right? One scratched me up when I was eight, and I haven't trusted them since. I won't ask your preference. It's real clear. So my question: morning person or night owl?"

"Morning easily. You?"

"Look who's being unoriginal now," he says. I roll my eyes. "Morning, too. I always get the best runs in first thing in the morning. Chocolate or vanilla?"

"Chocolate for sure," I say.

"That's why you've been staring at me so hard? All this chocolatey goodness over here?"

My mouth drops, and Micah cracks up. "You walked right into that one," he says.

"Jackass," I say, and he only laughs more. "PlayStation or Xbox?"

"Play. Stay. Tion. All day, every day, forever," Micah says. "You play?"

"Yep. I've got Call of Duty on lock. My brother, Junior, and I play online a couple of times a week. My sister joins every now and then, but the time difference makes it hard."

"Damn," Micah says, with a small smile. "I should start calling you New York."

"New York?"

"Yeah. I keep discovering new things I like about you, just like I do with the city."

My cheeks get warm, and it's got nothing to do with the heat wave.

This is the problem. I can easily fall into a "normal" with Micah before I realize it, which is a disaster waiting to happen when my boyfriend is only four seats away.

No, I can't do this. I can't. I hop up. "Um, you know what? I should probably . . . I should probably find a new seat."

Micah frowns. "What? Why?"

I grab my backpack. "I just need some space."

Someone takes a gentle hold of my arm. "Kay?" Tre'Shawn says. "You all right? He ain't messing with you, is he?"

"Wow. You really bugging," Micah says. "You act like you scared *I'll* scoop her up."

"Ain't nobody worried 'bout your nosy ass," Tre'Shawn says. "You need to stop speaking on things that don't concern you."

Mrs. Tucker is out of her seat and stepping between me and Tre'Shawn and Micah. "Everyone, back to your seats!"

"I care 'bout Kayla, so this does concern me," Micah says.

"Kayla ain't your concern!" says Tre.

I break away from his grasp and I put my hands up. "You know what? You two can figure this out on your own. Mrs. Tucker, I'm going downstairs."

Micah and Tre'Shawn both call after me, but I ignore them and climb down to the main level of the bus.

It's deserted down here. I'm not surprised. Like I said, all the other tourists got off a while ago and walked. Only the driver, Mr. Wright, is down here now. He nods and hums with an old R&B song on the radio. Hard to believe this is the same man who cusses people out so easily.

"Ah! Hello, my dear," he says, with that thick Jamaican accent. "Did that bossy woman up there send you down here to check on me now?"

I smirk and take the seat behind him. Bossy is an under-statement when it comes to Mrs. Tucker. She power trips to the highest degree. "No, sir. I wanted a different view, I guess."

"But the best view of the city is up there!" he says. "We're about to pass City Hall, in fact. You tourists love to see that place." He picks up his mic and tells the whole bus.

I shrug. "It's just another building to me."

He chuckles heartily, and I smile. His laugh reminds me of my dad's.

"You've got that right," he says. "It's just another building at the end of the day."

I settle into my seat and stare out the window. The blanket of darkness hasn't lifted from the city, yet it seems like everyone's already made good with the new normal. That's one thing I like about New Yorkers. They roll with the punches like they never feel the contact.

I take a deep breath. The situation with Tre'Shawn, the possibilities with Micah, the reveal with Jazmyn, they've all been suffocating me. Never thought I'd almost feel relieved to be by myself. Now the question is: What do I do?

"You wanna know something?" Mr. Wright says. "Tourists fawn over the city. Manhattan, Manhattan, Manhattan," he mocks. "But you haven't seen New York City until you've visited Brooklyn."

"You sound like my uncle. He lives there."

"Eh, is that so?" he says, eyeing me in the rearview mirror. "Which neighborhood?"

I shrug again.

"Oh no, no, no. You gotta know the neighborhood. Neighborhoods make all the difference, my dear. I live in Bed-Stuy."

I tilt my head. "Like that old rapper?"

"Old rapper? Oh, no, no, no." He shakes his head. "You can never step into Brooklyn and refer to Biggie Smalls in that manner. No, no, no."

"Biggie. Right." My bad for not remembering the name of a rapper who died before I was born. "I think my uncles and my cousins live in Bed-Stuy."

"And they didn't teach you no better than that? Bomboclaat!"

That sounded like a curse word. "I haven't seen them since I was a kid. I hoped I'd get to visit them during this trip, but that's probably not happening."

"Why not? You could catch a train."

"Mr. Wright, you've met my teacher," I say.

He laughs again. "Understood. If I could, I'd drive you over the bridge myself right now. There's supposedly a big block party in Bed-Stuy tonight. It'd give you southern kids a real taste of New York."

"Yeah, if only," I mutter, and sigh. My life is full of "if onlys" at the moment.

In the rearview mirror, I see Mr. Wright tilts his head while staring at me. "Something on your mind, dear?"

"I'm okay, but thank you," I say. This man has to navigate a double-decker bus through Manhattan. He doesn't need to hear about my problems.

"Child, you may as well spill it," he says. "It's written all over your face. Is it a boy? Or a girl? Or a nonbinary person?"

I'm impressed at his openness. Back home, I probably wouldn't get that benefit. "It's a boy. Two boys, actually."

"A love triangle," he says. "Those can be messy."

I hold my forehead. It's starting to ache just at the thought of this mess. "Yeah, and I've got an inkling it may actually be a love square."

He winces. "Ohhhhh. Quadruple messy."

"Right. I don't know what to do."

Which is a foreign feeling. I always know what to do to solve a problem. It's part of being an expectations meeter – nobody expects me to end up in bad situations because I always make the right choices.

This is totally different from choosing to not get pissy drunk at a party or picking an elective that will look good on my college applications. Hearts are involved. But unfortunately, I don't even know what mine wants. Tre'Shawn and Micah have both wiggled their way into little compartments inside of it.

"I may not know details, dear, but I have some advice if you'd like it," Mr. Wright says.

"I'll take whatever advice I can get, to be honest."

"If only my children started saying that." He chuckles. "Now, I'm going to assume that you don't know which of these young men you should be with, right?"

"Yes, sir."

"It's been a long time since I was around your age, so I may sound like an old man by saying this, but why do you have to choose?"

Umm . . . I know New York is a bit more eccentric than Mississippi, but is he saying what I think he's saying? "So I should be with both of them?"

"No, no!" Mr. Wright laughs. "Although nowadays that is an option, but that's not what I'm suggesting. I'm saying that maybe instead of choosing one of them, you could choose yourself, my dear. No one says you have to be in a relationship."

I bite my lip. "Even though I have feelings for them both?"

"All the more reason to give yourself time," he says. "Your heart will never lead you wrong, but it can be hard to hear it. You have to give it space to speak. That's a form of love, too."

Footsteps thump against the staircase, and seconds later Tre'Shawn's long legs make their way down them. He dips his head to see me. "Kay? You all right?"

I catch Mr. Wright's eyes in the rearview mirror. He mouths three words: *Help your heart.*

"Yeah," I tell Tre'Shawn. "I'm getting there."

He gives Mr. Wright a polite smile and sits beside me. "What's going on? For real?"

I put my hand on top of his on the seat. My adorable, loving, cheesy boyfriend with the soft hands, bad dance move, and dimples.

"I think that deep down, you know what's going on," I say.

"Huh? No, I don't."

"Yeah, you do," I say. "Look, I'm not coming at you about lying, okay? But ask yourself *why* you lied. You said you didn't wanna break my heart, but . . ." I swallow the lump in my throat. It's been there for a while, along with a truth I didn't wanna face. "But I wouldn't have been heartbroken over you not wanting to stream TV shows with me, Tre. You wanted space, and you think that's what would've broken my heart."

"Kayla—"

"It's okay if you did," I say over him. "I promise, it's okay. But if you love me, just admit it. This wasn't about a show, was it?"

He casts his eyes down, and he slightly shakes his head, as if he's arguing with himself.

But after a while he quietly says, "No. It wasn't about that. Shit," he hisses. "Kay, I'm sorry. That's foul as fuck —"

"It's okay, Tre. I want space, too."

He looks up at me. "What?"

"Yeah," I say, with a small smile that makes zero sense at a moment like this. "Lately, I've been thinking about how much everyone expects us to stay together. I wonder if that's why we're still together."

"Nah, Kay. I love you."

"I love you too," I murmur. "It's hard for me to imagine myself not being with you, and that . . . that scares me. I don't know who I am if I'm not your girlfriend. I don't think it should be that way."

Tre takes my hand in his and gently rubs his thumb along my palm.

"It shouldn't be," he says.

We don't say anything for a while, allowing New York to fill in the silence.

Fact: Micah did something to me, and I'm realizing that it goes beyond the feelings I caught for him. He helped me see that there are so many possibilities for me, for my heart. Forget what anyone expects: the only person I have to truly worry about is me.

To be honest, I don't know what I want right now. But like Mr. Wright says, maybe I should give my heart some space.

"Change is good," I murmur.

Tre'Shawn kisses my cheek. "Yeah. It is."

I rest my head on his shoulder. This doesn't feel like a breakup, just a break.

"Damn," Tre'Shawn says, after a minute. "Remember how

we used to plan our fantasy trip to New York?"

I laugh. "It didn't include a blackout, that's for sure."

"You wanted to see the Statue of Liberty and the Empire State Building, right? And ride over the –"

"The Brooklyn Bridge," I say. "Yeah. My parents walked over it once during a blackout. My mom was pregnant with me, in fact."

"For real? Dang. It would be dope if we could go see it somehow."

Mr. Wright clears his throat. "Not to stick my nose into matters that don't concern me, but I could make a wrong turn here or there and get you to the bridge. Maybe even to that block party I told you about, dear."

Tre'Shawn sits up a little. "Block party?"

"Don't even," I say, 'cause I see him getting excited. "There is no way Mrs. Tucker will let us go to a block party in a blackout."

"Who says she has to know that that's where we're going?" Mr. Wright asks.

Tre'Shawn laughs into his fist. "Yoo. What if we pull up at the party and convince her to let us stay? We can say it's some kinda cultural festival."

"For you southerners, a New York block party *is* a cultural festival," Mr. Wright adds.

I don't know if I'm offended or impressed. But I gotta admit– "That might work."

Mr. Wright makes a turn. "Oh, would you look at that.

Seems like I'm going in the wrong direction and headed toward Brooklyn."

Tre'Shawn and I laugh. He gives my hand a little squeeze.

Who knows, maybe in a couple of months people will be back to combining our names and expecting us to be together forever. Maybe we will be. Or maybe I'll end up with Micah.

I don't know. But for now, I'm fine with being just Kayla.

THE LONG WALK
ACT 5

Tiffany D. Jackson

The Brooklyn Bridge, 9:46 p.m.
The Brooklyn Bridge is nothing more than a shadow hovering above the East River, haunting and ghostlike with the lights off as hundreds of stranded Brooklynites flock to the footpath, trying to make it back home.

Kareem and I watch from the park across the street, near the City Hall station. Trains still down. I tried to call Dad but when he's working his bus route, he rarely answers the phone. "So. Now what?"

Kareem raises an eyebrow with a chuckle. "What you mean? Now we walk."

I look back at the sweaty heard of zombies, turtle-walking through the darkness, shoulder to shoulder. Men's ties undone, women limping in their heels, armpits soaked, moaning.

In the film world, we would call this the climax of the movie. The part where the protagonist meets and faces off with the antagonist in an ultimate battle between good and evil.

And here she is. Ready to kill me.

My mouth dries as the tremors in my chest rattle my core.

"Welp," I say with a wave. "It was nice seeing you again!"

I spin around, power walking away as Kareem chases after me, laughing.

"Girl, what you doing? We almost home!"

"I am not crossing that bridge. Hell no!"

He jumps in front of me, blocking my path. "Why?"

"You know why!"

Kareem stares, baffled, until it finally dawns on him and he slaps his forehead. "Heights! You're afraid of heights! Shit, I forgot."

"Yeah, soooo . . . later."

I try to walk off and he pins my shoulders.

"Is that why you've been dragging your feet this whole time? You didn't want to cross the bridge? Why didn't you say something?"

I open my mouth to defend my point but come up empty.

"Come on, Tammi, it'll be quick. I promise. We'll walk mad fast. Run if we have to!"

Eyes filling with tears, I choke back a sob. "I can't!"

He holds both of my hands, bending to meet my eye.

"Yes, you can. Just think of it as . . . one of our walks. We'll play, um, spot the wig! Or . . ." He looks down at my shoes. "Air Max!"

A chuckle escapes me. Kareem always made up little games for our long walks. One day we were spotting all the brownstones that had red doors, the next we were playing "count the gentrifiers."

"Air Max?" I scoff.

"Yeah. You got this! Besides, this is the only way. Okay?"

I take some deep breaths, looking back at my two worst nightmares merged into one: a crowd of people crossing over a bridge suspended in air. But beyond the bridge is home. Kareem is right; we're so close I can almost smell my mother's perfume. I have to try.

"Can you . . . hold my hand?"

Kareem blinks in surprise. "Yeah. Sure. I can do that."

Slowly, we merge into the steady stream of people and onto the walkway ramp, leaving Manhattan behind. In an instant, my chest tightens, heart pounds. Up ahead is the first of the two arches, with a web of steel cables supporting it.

"Just keep your eyes on the ground," Kareem whispers, hand sweaty in mine. "Look, see, over there? Air Max, white on white. Oh, and over to the right, homegirl got the army green. Or maybe they black."

I divert my eyes to the ground, focusing on all the shoes. Can this bridge even support all of us? What if someone falls off? I don't know how to swim!

"That's it, you're doing good," Kareem says, gripping my hand tighter. "Almost home."

A low hum of muttering fills my ears, the people in the crowd talking among themselves.

"I was stuck underground for over two hours," a woman ahead of us says, winded. "They made us walk through the tracks. Never been so scared in my life."

"I crossed the bridge like this before, during 9/11. Right after the second tower fell," a man says behind us. "So many people, felt like the bridge started to sway. Some even took off running."

Kareem whips his head around. "Yo, chill with all that talk, man! You trying to freak everyone out?"

The ground is spinning. Not the ground, the bridge. Made of wood and bricks that could drop us all into the river at any moment. My knees are Jell-O. I'm about to pass out as my chest heaves.

"I . . . can't," I gasp, waving a hand. "Can't. Breathe. Oh God!"

Kareem wraps an arm around my back, holding me up as the tears spill faster.

"Hey, hey, hey, you okay?"

Torn between running back onto land or staying frozen in my spot, I move to the side, and crumple into a pile, clutch a steel beam.

"No . . . no . . . no . . ." I whimper. "Is the bridge swaying? Is it moving?"

"Nah! It's not. I swear. Chill, okay? Just trust me."

Trust him? How can I trust him, anyone, or anything in this world?

"Just go, Kareem!" I wail, startling the people around us. "Go to your party with all your new friends and new girl! Just go!"

"Man, fuck a party! I'm not leaving you! Not like this."

My trembling hands clutch the metal tighter. "I'm scared! Please, no."

Kareem ropes me into a hug that feels life-changing. "Okay! Okay! It's aight. Let's just . . . over there! There's a bench over there. Come on!"

"No! I can't, can't . . . can't move."

Kareem lifts me up by the waist with one arm, carrying me over to the bench. "Here. Sit. Breathe. Deep breaths, remember? Like Ms. Kelly taught you."

My lungs clench as I try to sip up air, grabbing fistfuls of his shirt to ground myself. Ms. Kelly was our nurse in middle school who first taught me how to breathe when I get like this. Kareem was there every time.

"Ain't you supposed to put your head between your legs?" Kareem asks.

I nod, assuming the position, hugging my thighs as I watch a parade of shoes pass by. I spot a gray pair of Air Max. Even a leopard pair. I keep counting as my breathing eases. Grounding, that's what it's called. Kareem is quiet beside me, rubbing circles into my back. He's done this before. A few times. Every one of our walks was some type of distraction to keep me from falling apart.

After a few minutes, I sit up, the world spinning.

"Easy," Kareem coaches.

I take in our surroundings, noticing we've barely made it to the bridge's first arch. "Thanks," I whisper.

He chuckles. "Girl, how you expect to go to Atlanta if you can't even do heights?"

"Buses and trains still work, don't they?" I mumble.

He chuckles. "Man, you stubborn. And . . . beautiful."

My back straightens and I meet his gaze, drying tears.

Unbelievable. Even now, when I'm at my lowest . . .

"Fine, Kareem," I snap, shoving him away. "Just fine! You can have the internship, okay?"

"What?"

"That's why you're being all nice to me, right? You think you slick, but it's whatever. I don't care anymore. Take it!"

Kareem stares at me, a sadness in his eyes. "Is that what you think?" He shakes his head. "Damn, Tammi. Even after everything . . . why can't you just trust me?"

He folds his hands, leaning against his knees. Guilt hits me in the throat. There's that word again – *trust*. And now . . . it just doesn't make sense. Every time I've had a panic attack, he's never judged me, never told a soul, not even his mom. I trusted him with that and he never disappointed me. He was always supportive of everything, so why couldn't I be just as supportive for him? Why couldn't I trust him?

He's a pretty boy. You can't trust those types.

No! He's not "those types" and he never was. He's Kareem. I know him better than anyone. I should've never let anyone make me doubt him.

"I'm sorry. I didn't mean it like that." I sigh. "You should take the job."

"It's aight," he huffs, not meeting my eye. "You got into that special program, right?"

"Yeah, but you're right. You *do* know me. I *am* just running away. But I don't want to anymore. Not from you. Kareem, you were more than my boyfriend. You were my best friend and I . . . didn't trust you. You deserve better than that. So, you should take it. It's the least I can do. You need the money for St. John's, right?"

He frowns. "Huh? I'm not going to St. John's."

"Isn't that where Imani is going?"

"No idea. Me and Imani been done since graduation. Didn't your mom tell you?"

MOM! Of all the times to follow the rules!

"Oh. I'm . . . sorry?"

He shrugs. "It's cool."

I try to ignore the flutter in my heart at that piece of good news, forcing my smile back.

"Still, you should take the Apollo job, Kareem. I know you need the money for school. Wherever you end up going. And I know this city makes you happy and you want to stay. I . . . want you to be happy."

Kareem looks off into the distance, at the city skyline, still covered in darkness like a strange painting.

"I'm going to Clark Atlanta," he says.

I whip my head around to face him. "What? Why didn't you say something earlier?"

He shrugs, smirking. "We always said we'd go to school together, right?"

"Yeah but . . . things changed."

"Not everything. I know it's mad stalkerish but . . . I couldn't let you go down there alone." He laughs. "Real talk, I wasn't expecting to see you today, thought I'd have more time to get my game together. Was planning that ice cream move closer to homecoming."

There's a tenderness in his eyes. Has it been there all day?

Stuff like this only happens once in a lifetime and you won't take a second to just. Look. Up.

"You . . . still want to be with me? Even after everything I said in that message? Even after . . . all this?"

Kareem leans in, wrapping his arms around me. "Why wouldn't I?"

I burst into tears. "Because I'm a mess, Kareem! I can't even cross a damn bridge. I never leave the house and I don't do parties or crowds and you're, like, really cute, you should be with girls who—"

"But you're *my* mess. I rather have this mess every day than not at all."

"What about the other girls?"

"Why would I want other girls when I want you? Dummy!"

I blink and we bust out laughing.

That's the thing about finding the right person to love. When someone loves you, all their hang-ups don't really mean much. Because loving that person is a choice you have to make every day, even when that day isn't what you expect.

So I grab his shirt, pull him close, and kiss him. I kiss my messy, forgetful, silly-ass ex-boyfriend. And as we hover over the water, I forget the world as he kisses me back.

"Damn." He chuckles, knuckles grazing my jaw. "We should kiss on bridges more often."

I laugh until I notice a strange glow framing him like a halo, and gasp.

"Kareem, look! The lights are back on!"

Kareem spins around and just like that, the city has come back to life. Every building is now distinguishable.

"Whoa! They are!" He turns in the opposite direction. "But . . . don't look like they back on in Brooklyn. Maybe it takes a little longer."

I snuggle my head into the crook of his neck, and he kisses my forehead as we stare at the city skyline, taking in the view of my gorgeous city I could never be sick of. "It's pretty."

"Yeah," he agrees. "I was gonna say not as pretty as you but that's mad corny."

I laugh, feeling more comfortable than I have all day, even while hovering over the East River.

"Kareem?"

"Yeah?

"Think we can still make that party?"

He smirks. "Only one way to find out."

Kareem takes my hand and we walk the rest of the way. Together.

SEYMOUR AND GRACE

Nicola Yoon

Brooklyn, 10:05 p.m.

[Philosophy Now! PODCAST]

ANNOUNCER: On today's episode of the pod we're tackling one of the big ones: the question of identity. What makes you you?

Let's start the discussion by examining the parable of the Ship of Theseus, also known as Theseus's Paradox. Now, maybe it's been a long time since high school and you've forgotten who Theseus was, so let me bring you up to speed. In Greek mythology, Theseus was the legendary king of Athens. He was a big-time hero, but what he was most known for is defeating the Minotaur – the half-man, half-bull creature – in the Labyrinth of Crete.

In one version of the legend, after Theseus defeated the Minotaur, he sailed back home to Athens on a ship. His people were so overjoyed by his triumph they decided to honor him by preserving his ship in the harbor. Years passed and, over time, the ship started to deteriorate. In order to preserve the ship, his people would replace the parts, swapping out damaged planks for undamaged ones. After a thousand years of repair, all parts of the ship had been swapped out until none of the original parts remained.

Let me say that again: none of the original parts remained.

Now the question for you, my fellow philosophers, is this: after a thousand years, is the ship of Theseus sitting in the harbor still the Ship of Theseus?

If you answer no, then when did it stop being the Ship of Theseus? When the first plank of wood was replaced? The second? The last?

If you answer yes, then can I just build a ship using the old planks of wood and call that the Ship of Theseus?

GRACE

I stop texting Lana and lean forward in my seat. "Hey, do you mind turning that down a little?" I ask my Ryde driver.

He catches my eye in the rearview mirror. I give him a half smile so he knows I'm not trying to be a jerk. I could just turn it down myself. After all, Ryde's company motto is Where the Ryder Controls the Ryde. But messing with his radio just seems rude.

Still, there's no earthly reason for his radio to be on so loud with a passenger in his car.

"Guess you're not a fan of philosophy," he says.

Am I imagining the attitude in his voice? I admit I'm in a Mood and feeling sensitive right now. Maybe I'm not taking things the way they're meant.

"It's just a little loud," I say. Diplomatically.

"Sure. You need to concentrate on your texting. No doubt

your emojis are saving the world."

Okay, so the attitude is not my imagination. "Excuse me?" I say. I know how to make my voice so frosty it freezes people right up.

But he doesn't freeze.

He gives me another quick look in the rearview mirror. "Were you listening?" he asks. "It's a great podcast. It's called Philosophy Now! The Ship of Theseus parable is basically asking how much a person can change and still be considered the same person."

My phone buzzes with another text from Lana.

> LANA: !!!!!
> LANA: Just spotted him!
> LANA: You leave your house yet?
> LANA: When are you getting here?!

The "here" is the block party I'm going to. The "him" is my ex-boyfriend, Derrick, the whole reason I'm even going to this party. We dated for almost two years. Six weeks ago, he broke up with me.

I switch my camera to selfie mode and make sure I look as good as when I left the house. Not that it even matters how I look. With the blackout still going, it's not like he'll be able to see me properly.

The driver starts up again. "It's the problem of identity," he says. "We're not the same person we were ten years ago, five years ago, or even yesterday. We like different foods. We don't love the people we used to love, and they don't love us."

That last part – "We don't love the people we used to love, and they don't love us" – makes me look up from my phone.

He turns to look at me for a quick second. I don't see his face for long enough to be sure-sure, but I'm pretty sure he's kind of hot.

"We don't share anything in common with our old selves. So why do we say we're the same people?" he asks.

It's kind of an interesting question. Ordinarily I would be into it, but right now I'm too busy trying to decide what I'm going to say to Derrick once I see him.

Lana texts again. Apparently, Trish, the girl who has been in a lot of Derrick's social media posts lately, is there now. It's not like I'm going to this party to try to get him back by reminding him of what we used to have. Okay, it's exactly like that. I know how pathetic it sounds, but I'm hoping he'll take one look at me and regret breaking us up.

It's going to take us forever and a day to get to this party. The blackout has been going on for hours now, and every stoplight we pull up to is not working because of it. Cars are taking turns inching through the intersections.

"Want to hear something even wilder?" my driver asks.

I wave my phone at him. "Sorry, I don't really have time for this. Could you please turn down –"

But he just keeps going. "We change out every one of our cells, all our everything, every seven years. My current body doesn't share a single cell in common with my two-year-old body," he says. "If your current self is not the same as your past self, then what's the point of planning for anything? Our future selves will be nothing like us. Different tastes, different friends, different cells. Our future self is a complete stranger, a totally different person. So, why do we spend all this time making plans and doing things for a person we don't even know?"

He's so busy philosophizing, he doesn't realize the car ahead of us has moved. The car behind us honks long and loud. The sound makes him jump in his seat and hit the gas a little too hard.

I navigate to my Ryde app. The driver's name is Seymour. I consider giving him a one-star rating. What would I write in the comment? Driver is having an existential crisis.

Instead of one-starring him, I decide to take advantage of the company motto. I use the app to turn off his podcast and start my Abba playlist.

The opening lyrics of "Knowing Me, Knowing You" fills the car.

My driver starts laughing. "Guess that's my hint to stop talking," he says.

I stare out the window. It's just after 10:00 p.m., but the blackout makes it seem later than it is. The streetlamps are off and all the storefronts are dark. Every so often a car headlight or someone's phone will land on a storefront or a person's face, and the sudden spotlight somehow makes ordinary things seem different and surprising. I wonder if Derrick will seem different when I see him.

Lana texts again.

> LANA: They're dancing
> LANA: No body parts are touching
> LANA: Yet

I tilt my head back against the seat, squeeze my eyes closed, and try not to worry about what their dancing means.

My driver starts singing along with Abba. His voice is so terrible it's actually funny. He's not anywhere close to hitting the right notes. I lean back in my seat and sing along with him. My voice doesn't falter – not even when I get to the line about how breaking up is never easy.

SEYMOUR

Three Abba songs in and I'm looking for a way to escape my own car. Serves me right for aggravating a classic prima donna passenger with my philosophizing. (Prima donnas are one of the four most difficult types of passengers. The others are:

The Sociopath – sits in the front passenger seat next to you, but doesn't talk;

The Bro – insists you play whatever music you want, and assumes that what you want to play is rap. Name-drops Tupac and Biggie. Is unaware that they are both dead. Overdances in the back seat to show that he is down. Only guys do this.

White guys;

The Demon Child – kicks the back of your seat repeatedly. If you hold them down and check, you'll find 666 written just behind the ear.

Prima donnas are girls like this one now – pretty and buttoned-up. No hello or eye-contact when they get in the car. Monosyllabic responses. Looking down at their phones like the meaning of life is on there.)

This girl is prettier than your average prima donna, though. She's beautiful – dark brown skin; long, skinny dreads; big eyes; and full lips that tilt up at the corners. She looks like she smiles a lot. She's funny too. I'm pretty sure she played "Knowing Me, Knowing You" because my podcast was about identity.

No doubt she's going to give me a one-star rating if she hasn't done it already. Maybe I should say sorry or something. I know I'm only giving her a hard time because my fight with Tommy last night is still bugging me. I need to find my way to a better mood though. I can't afford to bring my rating down. I need this job.

The Ryde map says it's going to take about an hour to get this girl to where she's going. Usually this trip would take thirty minutes max. With the lights out, though, traffic is so backed up this street might as well be a parking lot. I hope she has other songs on her playlist. An hour is a long time to listen to Abba.

I take another peek at her in the rearview. The light from her phone makes her face glow. Now that she's not trying to get me to shut up, I can see she looks sad.

I wonder what her life story is. When I first took this job, one of the perks for me was I'd get to know people from all over the city, from all walks of life. I had this idea that my car would be some kind of a bubble where people could hit pause on their busy lives. I'd get them talking, and maybe learn something essential about people and life.

But mostly people don't want to talk. Everyone in here is just on their way to someplace else. Caught up in the drama of their own lives. We intersect for a short time, and then go our separate ways. Sometimes I just want to hold on to people and make them stay.

"What did you say?" Prima donna asks from the back seat.

I catch her eyes in the rearview. "You talking to me?" I ask.

"I thought you were talking to me. You said something about making people stay."

"My bad," I say. "I do that sometimes. Say the thing in my head out loud."

"Okay, then," she says, and goes back to looking out into the dark.

My phone rings. It's Tommy calling for the sixth time today. I let it go to voicemail. A few seconds later my phone lights up with a text. Another few seconds after that, he calls again.

"You mind if we give Swedish pop sensation Abba a rest so I can take this?" I ask.

"It's fine," she says with a little laugh.

I do a quick turn in my seat so I can catch what she looks

like laughing. She looks . . . good.

I put in my earbuds and pick up. "Tommy, what's up?"

"I've been calling and calling you, man," he says.

"Yeah, been away from my phone most of the day." I don't know why I bother to lie. Easier than telling him I don't want to talk, I guess.

It's a few seconds before he says anything. "Sorry about what I said last night, man. I didn't mean nothing by it."

I don't say anything, because of course he meant something by it. Words mean things.

"You want to hang later?" he asks.

"I can't, man. Working." I can hear him wanting to say something else. "Listen, I can't talk now. I'm about to pick up a Ryde."

I hang up, pull my earbuds out, and toss them on the passenger seat.

Up until this past year, Tommy and I were as close as brothers. We met in fifth grade because our parents were friendly with each other. They're from Jamaica, same as mine. We've been through everything together. Our lives have always been on the same track, both of us following the plan our parents had for us: do good in high school, get at least one scholarship and some financial aid, and go to one of the state schools they could afford. But then last year, he went off to Binghamton University while I stayed here doing this job. Nothing's been the same between us since.

I give a quick honk to the cabbie in front of me to get him

moving. I think he might've been sleeping. I half turn to the girl. "Sorry about the call," I say. "You can start your music back up."

"It's okay," she says. "Go ahead and put your podcast back on."

"For real? How come?"

She shrugs. "Sorry I turned it off before. I'm having a crappy day." She looks away and then back at me again. "Anyway, you seem like your day is as bad as mine," she says.

That's nice of her. Maybe she's kinder than your average Primadonna. "So, where you headed?" I ask.

"Block party. I'm meeting my boyfriend there," she says. She emphasizes boyfriend the way girls do when they're warning you off.

I laugh to myself. One of my little sisters, Serena, does the same thing. As far as all the boys in her high school know, she has a serious long-distance boyfriend in Ghana.

"You from Jamaica?" I ask. "I thought I heard a little accent."

"You can hear that?" she says, surprise in her voice.

"My folks are from Mobay. I'd recognize that accent anywhere. How long ago did you move here?"

"Two years ago. I was sixteen."

Something in her voice makes me ask: "You miss it?"

She looks out her window. "Yeah. Most of my family is still there. My friends."

I can hear the longing in her voice. I wonder if she's still close with her friends. Two years is a long time.

People lose each other in shorter amounts of time than that. I know that from experience.

GRACE

Lana hasn't texted in a few minutes. No doubt she and Tristán are kissing their faces off since she finally, finally told him how she feels about him. It turns out he's been in love with her this whole time too.

I need to distract myself so I don't obsess about what may or may not be happening with Derrick and Trish. So I don't obsess over what she has that I don't.

I turn my phone facedown and look over at my driver. "How come you were listening to that podcast?" I ask.

"I just think it's interesting," he says with a shrug. He doesn't seem as eager to talk about it as he was before he got that phone call.

"Well, I disagree with what you were saying," I say.

That perks him up. He turns and gives me a quick look and a smile. "Which part?" he asks.

"It doesn't matter if my body and all my cells are completely different than they used to be," I say. "I'm still the same person. My body may have changed, but my memories haven't. I remember who I was yesterday, and I'll know who I am tomorrow."

He gives me an even bigger smile. I get the feeling that he loves debating esoteric stuff like this. I have to admit I like it too. I can't imagine Derrick wanting any part of a conversation like this.

"So if it turns out I'm a terrible driver and we get into an accident right now and you get amnesia, then you're no longer the same person?" he asks.

"I'd still be the same person, just with amnesia," I say.

"Are you sure? Because now you really don't have anything in common with your pre-accident self. You don't have the same body. You don't have the same cells. You don't even have the same memories. Nothing."

I lean forward into the space between our seats. "So the question is: What makes you *you*?"

"Exactly," he says, tapping on the steering wheel for emphasis.

"Well, do you have an answer?"

He laughs and shakes his head. "Nope."

"Doesn't that drive you bonkers?" I ask.

"Nope," he says. "I like asking the questions."

He turns to smile at me just as headlights from another car shine right into ours. I feel my eyes get cartoon-character wide as my brain processes how cute he is. Warm brown skin, big dark eyes, and cheekbones for days. He's got one of those faces that belongs on a billboard.

I look away from him and then back again, but he's already facing forward. I study the back of his head and his profile. It turns out you can't tell how good-looking a person is based on the back of their head and profile. "How old are you, anyway?" I ask.

"Just turned nineteen a few days ago."

"Happy belated birthday."

He smiles at me in the rearview. "Thanks."

We pull up to an intersection and he flicks on the turn signal.

"Are you listening to that for college or something?" I ask.

He doesn't answer for a while, just rubs his thumb on the steering wheel. The ticktock of the turn signal sounds even louder in the quiet.

Finally, he says, "I'm not in college." He takes a deep breath. "My pops passed away two years ago." His voice is so quiet I almost don't hear him.

"I'm really sorry," I say.

"Thanks, I appreciate that," he says. "You'd be surprised how many people don't know what to say after you tell them a thing like that. Anyway, the plan was always for me to go to Binghamton. After Pops died, I couldn't just leave my mom alone to take care of my sisters. And with him gone, money got tight. Moms is the type to take on two, three, four extra jobs to make ends meet, but I can't have her running herself ragged. Better for me to stay here and take this job and let the college thing go."

I don't know what to say, so I just say I'm sorry again.

"You know that phone call I got earlier?"

"You mean the one you didn't want to take, but then you did take and then couldn't wait to get off of?"

"That's the one," he says, laughing.

He tells me all about his friend Tommy. They grew up together and were supposed to have the same life, but because of what happened with his dad, he stayed here while Tommy went off to college.

"We were out together last night, and we got into it. He wanted to go to some fancy club in the city with a huge-ass cover charge." He looks out his window and sighs. "I just wanted to hang out, play a video game like we used to. When I said I wanted to do something that didn't cost a lot, he said I was turning into an old man. Wanted to know when I got so cheap. Said I was different these days."

"No wonder you didn't want to take that call," I say.

"Yeah," he says, and then starts laughing to himself. "Sorry, I didn't mean to lay all this on you."

"It's okay," I say, laughing too. "People tell me things all the time. I have one of those faces."

"That and you're a good listener," he says. "Well, now that you know everything about me, I feel like I should officially introduce myself," he says. "My name is Seymour."

"I'm Grace," I say. "Do people make puns about your name all the time?"

"You mean things like 'Hey, Seymour, can you see more?'"

I grin. "Yeah, like that," I say.

Passing headlights flash a bar of light across his eyes.

"Never," he says, and grins at me through the rearview. "It's nice to meet you, Grace," he says.

SEYMOUR

She hasn't said anything since we introduced ourselves. I think I depressed her with all my talk about Pops and Tommy. If she didn't one-star me before, she's surely going to do it now.

"Driver is depressing as shit," she'll write in the comments.

I'm trying to think of a joke or something to lighten the mood, when my gas gauge beeps. I study the needle. It's definitely pointing to E(mpty).

Shit.

Was that the first this-is-just-a-warning beep? Or was it the third you-should-pull-over-now beep? I flick the gauge with my finger like that's going to move the needle back to Full.

"Please tell me you didn't just run out of gas," Grace says from the back seat.

"I didn't just run out of gas," I say, flicking the gauge again. "We have enough to make it to your party."

But the car starts to slow down as soon as the words are out of my mouth.

I feel her eyes burning into the back of my neck.

I need to make my way to the right lane so I can pull over. The only thing worse than running out of gas would be running out of gas in the middle of the street. Even though I signal to change lanes, the person behind speeds up and flips me off. People really think they own the piece of the road they're on.

Finally, I make it all the way over and turn off onto a residential side street. We're close to the Boerum Hill neighborhood. I don't know much about this part of Brooklyn except that it's fancy. Organic this. Artisan that. The sidewalks are tree-lined. The brownstones are huge and expensive looking. Only a few of them have candles flickering in the windows. Very few people are out on the sidewalk. It looks dark out here. Lonely.

I pull into a spot halfway in the red just in time for the car to sputter to a stop. I take my key from the ignition and peek at her in the rearview to get a sense of how mad she is. She's massaging her temples and taking deep breaths.

I turn around. "I'm an idiot," I say.

She narrows her eyes at me and gets out of the car without saying anything.

I get out too and catch up to her on the sidewalk. She's already back in the app, trying to get another Ryde.

"I'm the worst Ryde driver ever," I say. "You should definitely give me one-star. Actually, you should give me zero stars."

She looks up from her phone. "You can do that?" she asks.

"I was joking."

"Oh," she says. "You're being funny."

"Ouch," I say.

She shakes her head and goes back to the app. I doubt she's going to get lucky enough to find another Ryde at this hour with the blackout still going.

"Listen," I say, "your party is only a thirty-five-minute walk from here. Let me walk you over there."

She shakes her head. "I can walk by myself."

"But it's dark," I say.

"My feet still work in the dark," she says.

"I'm talking about your safety." I know I sound like an annoying older brother, but I don't care. "Do you know this neighborhood?"

"No," she admits, looking around. She folds her arms and

taps her foot. "But I don't know you either, so."

"Fair enough, so let me fix that," I say. "You already know something about my pops. His name was Walter. He was an English teacher. Loved philosophy and poetry. My mom's name is Carol and she's a history teacher. They met teaching at the same school in Jamaica before they moved here. I have two younger sisters. Serena's eight and Melanie is twelve." I take a quick pause to catch my breath and then keep going. "Now you know me a little and I'm begging you not to let me leave you out here by yourself when this situation is my fault. My mom would kill me. My sisters would kill me. Please let me walk you so I don't have to die at the hands of the women in my life."

She starts laughing. "Okay," she says. "But only because I don't want your death on my conscience."

I'm relieved and not just because she's letting me walk with her and help keep her safe. I'm relieved because now I get to keep talking with her for a little while longer.

She takes a picture of my license plate, and then one of me, and then one of me posing next to the license plate. "I'm texting this to my friend Lana," she says. "That way if I turn up dead, they'll know who did it."

I laugh as she maps out walking directions. For a few minutes, we walk without talking like both of us are adjusting to being in this new space together. In the distance I can hear fireworks going, like they've been doing since summer started. The sound echoes off the buildings, but they're too far away for me to catch a glimpse of.

We cross Atlantic Avenue onto another residential street. This one is lively, with neighbors mingling on the sidewalks or sitting on their stoops talking. The houses here are narrow, three-story brownstones that look a lot like the one I live in. Candles are everywhere, on windowsills and lining porch steps. There are lots of little kids chasing each other up and down the sidewalks with flashlights, pretending to be ghosts. Some people have even brought old-school boom boxes into the street. I hear everything from rap to pop to calypso to dancehall. It feels like a celebration. Like the blackout gave everybody an excuse to relax and be with each other.

Overhead, the moon is almost full. Which is great, because it gives off enough light for me to keep sneaking little glances at her. Man, she's pretty. Sometimes the moonlight catches on the beads in her dreads so she looks like she's glittering.

"Do you believe in signs?" she asks me.

"Like from God or the universe?"

"Yeah," she says. "Maybe this blackout and you running out of gas is a sign."

"Of what?"

"That I'm stupid to go to this party."

"How come you don't want to go?" I ask. "Didn't you say you're meeting your boyfriend there?"

"Ex-boyfriend," she says. "I only said boyfriend so you wouldn't hit on me." She side-eyes me. "You wouldn't believe how many guys think just because a girl is talking to him that must mean she's into him."

I have to stop walking so I can laugh properly. "I wasn't going to hit on you," I say, even though she's right. I definitely would've hit on her by now if she hadn't told me she had a boyfriend.

The look she gives me tells me she knows I'm lying.

"All right," I say. "Tell me about this ex-boyfriend situation." I make sure to emphasize the ex.

"No way," she says, shaking her head. "I'm not telling a complete stranger all about my love life."

"Come on. You're the one who said this night is a sign. Maybe the sign is that you should tell a complete stranger your problems so that he can solve them," I counter. "Besides, in thirty minutes, after I drop you off, we'll never see each other again."

My stomach does a funny little roll as soon as I say that last part. I don't like the idea of not seeing her again.

Another side-eye from her, but this time she looks like she's making a decision. "What do you want to know?"

"The whole thing," I say.

She tells me they started dating right after she moved to America and went out for almost two years. He befriended her right away, showed her the ropes of their high school, and introduced her to all his friends. He even introduced her to one of her best friends, Lana.

"What reason did he give for the break up?" I ask.

She gives me another skeptical why-am-I-talking-to-a-stranger look.

I give her my best your-secrets-are-safe-with-me look.

"He said things were good between us, but that it was time for us to move on."

"Jesus, what does that even mean?" This guy sounds like a real prize. And I'm not just saying that because I think she's smart and funny and beautiful and whatever.

She throws her hands up in the air. "That's what I said," she says.

"And what did he say?"

"He said we were going off to college soon and that long distance things don't work." She stops walking and looks up at the sky. "But that wasn't the real reason he broke up with me. When I pressed him, he said he just didn't love me anymore." She shakes her head like she's still trying to make sense of it. "He said I was different now. Like it was a bad thing."

"Who you are now seems pretty cool to me," I say, before I think better of it.

She ducks her head and laughs like I've embarrassed her.

"You know what's funny? That's the same thing Tommy said to me last night. That I was different now. But I'm the same. He's the one that's different."

"Maybe that's why you're so mad at him," she says.

"I'm not following you."

"Maybe what you're mad at is that he's living the life you were supposed to have. You were supposed to go off to college and come back different. You were supposed to come back with expensive tastes and new ideas in your head and thinking you know everything because you took a few classes."

I stop walking to stare at her. A white kid on a skateboard grinds by.

Is she right? Is that why I'm so angry? "You're saying I'm jealous of him?" I ask.

"I'm saying maybe you should let go of your old dreams and make new ones."

GRACE

Lana finally texts me back fifteen minutes after I sent her Seymour's picture and license.

> LANA: Holy hell, THAT guy is your Ryde driver?
> LANA: He's hot AF
> LANA: Not as hot as Tristan
> LANA: But still hot
> LANA: Hurry up and bring him here so I can get a better look at him
> LANA: Srsly, can't you walk any faster?

I laugh down at my phone. As it is, I'm already walking double-time to keep up with Seymour and his long legs.

What a weird way for this night to be turning out. I didn't expect to be walking the streets of Brooklyn in the dark telling my break-up story to a virtual stranger. He hasn't said very much since I said the thing about him making new dreams. I wonder if I pissed him off.

I check my phone. We're only twelve blocks away from

the party now. Another burst of fireworks goes off. Two little Black girls in matching red jumpers and matching afro poofs stop to look up at the sky. When they don't see anything, they focus on us instead and make loud, kissing sounds at us as they go laughing by.

Seymour and I look at each other and laugh too.

"I have an idea," he says. "You should practice your speech on me."

"What speech?" I ask.

"The one you're going to give to Derrick when you see him."

"I don't really have one."

He stops walking. "Come on. Pretend I'm him." He hunches over and sucks in his cheeks. "Is he shorter than me? Skinnier? Less good-looking?"

I shake my head, but play along anyway. "Hey, Derrick," I say.

"Hey, Grace, it's nice to see you," he says, but instead of using his regular voice, he uses the deep, dumb-guy voice that all girls use to make fun of their boyfriends.

I laugh. "How am I supposed to do this if you're not serious?"

"Okay, okay," he says. "Go on."

"How's your summer been going?"

"It's good. Not as good without you, though."

"Derrick would never say that," I say. "He's more the silent type." It's actually one of the things I liked least about him. He never said how he felt.

We come to a crosswalk. Traffic is so jammed we don't need

to wait for the light to cross. We just weave our way through the stopped cars.

"So, what about you?" I ask. "Do you have a girlfriend?"

"Nope. I'm a single man."

"Do you want a girlfriend or are you one of those guys who likes to date around?"

"I'm just waiting for the right one to come along," he says.

I like how sincere he is. "What's your type?" I ask, curious to know what the "right one" is.

"I don't really have a type," he says.

"Everybody has a type."

"You really want to know?" he asks, slowing down.

"Yes," I say. I want to know more than I expected to, actually.

He puts his hands in his pockets and takes a long pause like he's gearing up for something. "Okay, but you can't call me corny after I tell you," he says.

Now I'm dying to know. "Promise," I promise.

"I like girls who are curious."

"Wait. Curious . . . how?" I ask, needing to clarify just exactly what he's talking about here.

"Get your mind out of the gutter," he says, laughing. "Curious about the world, I mean. You know the podcast I was playing back in the car? I love that stuff. I love thinking about those big meaning of life questions. My pops was like that too. We'd sit on our front porch in these rocking chairs my mom bought. He'd drink his Red Stripe and I'd drink my pineapple soda and we'd talk about all sorts of things, just me and him."

He looks up at the sky. Moonlight makes his face shimmer silvery brown. He gives me a small smile. "Most people think talking about philosophy is dumb, like if you can't do anything practical with it, then what's the point of talking about it? But he didn't think that."

"He sounds like he was great," I say, looking up at the sky too.

"He really was," he says, with a small sigh. "Anyway, I like girls who'll get all geeky over stuff like that with me. Like when we were talking in the car, I could tell you were really getting into the Ship of Theseus stuff. And you're smart. You made some good points about how memory is part of identity. And I like what you said about the real reason I'm mad at Tommy and about me making new dreams for myself. You've made me laugh a bunch of times, too."

He stops talking and slaps his hand over his mouth, realizing what he's done. He basically just told me that I am his type.

"Damn," he says, looking down at his feet. "Swear to God I wasn't trying to hit on you there. I know you've got the Derrick thing going on. And even if you didn't, I probably shouldn't–"

"It's really okay. You don't have to apologize," I say, holding my hand up. "Anyway, it was a really nice thing to say."

His head snaps up. "Yeah?" he asks.

"Yeah," I say.

We smile at each other but then it gets awkward. I take out my phone again and check the directions, mostly so I can give both of us a minute to get it together. It's a good thing I do because it turns out we were supposed to turn right a block ago.

I'm about to tell him when he points at the gas station across the street. "You mind if we stop by there?" he asks. "Their pump lights are still on. Maybe they have a back-up generator and I could buy a canister of gas for the car."

We cross the street and I wait outside while he goes into the little store to talk to the clerk.

A few feet away from me, a fire hydrant is shooting water high into the sky. Three little Black boys, maybe nine or ten years old, are completely soaked and happily dancing in and out of the water.

Someone, maybe the older sister of one of them, is playing music from her phone and laughing at their antics. We smile at each other.

I watch the kids some more. Their skinny little legs fly everywhere. They're giggling in that free, wide-open way only little kids can, like the world is made for them, like nothing has ever been this good before.

The blackout makes the city feel like it's on hold, like someone hit a giant pause button. That's the way I've been feeling lately too, since Derrick broke up with me. Like I'm waiting for my life to start back up.

After a few minutes, Seymour comes out of the store carrying a red gas canister and five ice-cream cones. "The lady inside gave them to me for free," he says. "Said they're getting too soft to keep since the freezer isn't working."

He looks over at the maybe older sister. "Okay if I give these to the kids?" he asks.

"That is so sweet of you!" she says.

The little boys squeal as they take their cones, even happier now than they were before. One of them, the shortest one with enormous ears, sizes Seymour up. He looks at me. "That your boyfriend?" he asks me.

"Oh my God, Owen, that is none of your business," his maybe big sister says.

"It's okay," I tell her, laughing.

"No, Owen," I say, leaning close to him. "He's not my boyfriend." I think about explaining the Ryde situation, but decide against it. It feels like we're more than driver and passenger now.

"We're friends," I say. I can feel Seymour's eyes on me.

"Okay, then," Owen says, and dances away to the edge of the water, licking his cone.

"Friends?" Seymour says. "That mean you forgive me for running out of gas?"

"We're not there yet," I tease.

He laughs. "Tell me something about you then, get this friendship thing going."

I tell him that I'm an only child so it's just me and my parents. My dad is a sous chef at a fancy French place in Tribeca. My mom's an accountant. Their dream is to eventually open an upscale Jamaican restaurant.

"What do you miss most about Jamaica?" he asks.

When people ask me this question, I usually say something superficial – something they expect me to say – like my family or the beach or the food. And I do miss all of those things, but they're not what I miss the most.

"I miss feeling like I belong someplace," I say.

He nods slowly. "Yeah, I understand that," he says, and I get the feeling he really does.

More fireworks go off, and this time I catch a flash of red sparks from behind a building.

An older white couple holding hands walks toward us. "Beautiful night, isn't it?" says the man.

Seymour nods. "It's working out great," he says as they pass by.

SEYMOUR

We're less than a block away from her party now. The music is getting louder. I can already smell jerk chicken and pork from where we are. We keep walking until we're just at the edge of the party. It's packed with people laughing and dancing. It's like being in a big, open-air club where the lights are real low. The whole block has a slight orange glow to it from all the candles and lanterns that people have put out. Just like on the other street, I see more kids chasing each other with flashlights. There's even another fire hydrant going with some kids playing in it. Along the sidewalk, I see buckets of ice packed with beer and soda.

I stand there smiling at all the happiness, at how none of

these people have let the blackout stop them from having a good time. I remember what Grace said to me about getting some new dreams.

"Well, this is it," Grace says, and turns toward me.

"Thanks for letting me get you here safe," I say.

She laughs and looks around. "I can't believe the lights are still out."

I don't know what to say, but I want to say something so we can linger and talk more. "I'm glad they're still out," I say, wishing this weren't the end. Wishing I was going into this party with her.

Her phone buzzes.

I know it's time to let her get on with her life. "Guess I should go," I say. I jiggle the gas canister. "Gotta fill up and get back to it."

"Thanks again," she says.

I take a step back, but I can't quite make myself go, not without taking a chance.

"Lemme ask you something. You know how I basically confessed that you were my type?"

She puts a hand on her face. I think she might be blushing. "Yeah," she says.

"If it weren't for the Derrick situation, you think you'd like to spend some time with me debating esoteric philosophical podcasts about the nature of identity?"

She looks at me for a few seconds. She's backlit by candlelight and I could be happy just standing here staring at her for a long time. She starts to say something. But before she can, a girl comes barreling up to us. She's wearing a lot of jewelry, all of it jingling madly.

"Hi," says jewelry girl, giving me a once-over. "You the Ryde driver who doesn't understand cars need fuel?"

"That's me," I say, laughing. "You the sassy best friend?"

"The one and only," she says with a curtsey. "Thanks for escorting my girl."

"No problem," I say. I'm still looking at Grace, hoping she'll answer my question, even though I know in my heart that the moment's gone.

Her friend looks back and forth between us a few times. "Grace," she whisper-shouts. "Derrick's over in the jerk chicken line."

That's my cue to go. "It was nice running out of gas with you, Grace," I say. "Good luck with everything."

"You too," she says.

GRACE

I feel a little queasy watching him go. It's the same feeling I get when I realize – too late – that I got an answer wrong on a test.

He disappears into the crowd.

Lana snaps her fingers in front of my face. "What was that all about?" she asks.

"I think I just got hypothetically asked out."

"What did you hypothetically answer?"

"I didn't," I say and then change the subject before she can press me some more. "Where's Tristán?"

A mile-wide smile spreads across her face. "Somewhere getting me a soda," she says.

I pull her into a tight hug. "I'm really happy for you guys," I say.

A white guy doing some sort of weird interpretive dance accidentally bumps into us. Lana rolls her eyes at him and shuffles us over to the sidewalk where there are fewer people.

"You look great," she says. She adjusts my necklace and brushes my braids from my shoulders. "Ready for this?"

I grab her hand and squeeze it. "What am I doing again?"

"What is up with you?" she asks. "You're showing Derrick exactly what he's been missing. Isn't that what you want?"

I nod because she's right. That's what I've been saying I want for six weeks now. Except now I'm not so sure anymore. I don't know what I'm doing here or what I want to happen.

"The jerk truck is down there on the right," she says, pointing down the street. He stands near a red double-decker tour bus. Weird. She wishes me luck and then I'm off.

I weave my way through the crowd, saying lots of "excuse me"s and "I'm sorry"s. The whole time I try to think of what to say to Derrick. Should it be something nostalgic? Something to remind him why we used to go out in the first place?

But nothing occurs to me. Instead what pops into my head is Seymour doing his dumb-guy voice and encouraging me to practice my speech on him. I laugh and shake my head. He's funny.

Finally, I make it over to the truck. Even though I'm not hungry, the smoky, spicy jerk smell makes me want to order a plate or two.

I scan the line and spot Derrick close to the front. My heart thumps hard a couple of times, but then settles down. He looks different since the last time I saw him. He's tanned a nice, deep brown and he let his fade grow out. There's a dumb little goatee thing happening on his face. Except for that, though, he looks good.

I walk up to him, but he's looking down at his phone and doesn't notice me right away. "Hey, Derrick," I say.

His lifts his head in this sluggish way he has that always makes it seem like he's moving in slow motion. "Gracie," he says, and looks me up and down. "Wow, you look great."

"Thanks," I say. "You too."

We stand there awkwardly for a few seconds. He recovers first, smiles, and pulls me in for a hug. "It's nice to see you," he says. "How come you're here? You never used to like these things."

And that's when I finally figure it out – the problem with Derrick and me. The problem is that he wants me to be the same as I've always been. He wants me to stay the same shy girl, fresh off the plane from Jamaica, who didn't know anything or anyone. The girl who needed him for everything. He was right when he broke up with me. I am different. I have changed.

And that's not a bad thing.

Right then, a girl – Trish – comes up to us. I recognize her from Derrick's social media posts. Her eyes linger on Derrick's face, and it's obvious how much she likes him.

Finally, her eyes bounce back and forth between us. There's a nervous little frown on her face.

I rush to reassure her that she has nothing to worry about. "You're Trish, right?" I say, sticking my hand out to shake hers. "It's nice to meet you. Derrick was just talking all about you."

She beams. "He was?"

"He was," I say. She beams some more.

I turn to Derrick. "I gotta go, but it was nice running into you," I say. "I'll see you around."

He frowns and looks like he's going to say something else, but I'm already leaving. I duck back into the crowd and let myself get carried away for a minute.

Lana must've been keeping tabs on me, because suddenly she's right beside me. Tristán is with her now and wearing the same mile-wide smile that she is.

"You finally got yourself the right girl," I say.

He smiles even wider.

"Well?" Lana says, bouncing on her toes. "What happened with Derrick?"

"It was nice to see him," I say, still trying to work out exactly what I'm feeling.

"Nice to see him?" she says, imitating my voice. "Woman, didn't you just spend the last however many weeks telling me how much you miss him?"

"I know," I say, "but I think I was wrong."

"And you're just now realizing this?"

"Yes," I say.

"This is about that Ryde guy, isn't it? I saw the way he was looking at you."

I saw it too. He likes me. This version of me right here.

I hope I'm not too late. If I run, maybe I'll be able to catch up to him before he gets back to his car and leaves.

I tell her my plan. "Will you come with me?"

She looks at Tristán. "You mind?" she asks him.

He offers to come with us, but she tells him to stay and help Twig hype people up. They kiss goodbye and then she grabs my hand.

"Come on," she says.

We start squeezing our way through the crowd. It feels like the party has doubled or tripled in the last few minutes, like everyone in New York decided this was the place to be – partying in Brooklyn on a street lit only by candlelight and moonlight. Twig and another guy are on a platform bent over a pair of turntables. Twig closes his eyes, falling into a trance with the music while the other guy sticks out his tongue at the other Jamaican girl from my class, Tammi. She fails at holding in a laugh. Nearby, Nella is perched on a speaker, smiling down at a girl I don't know. They're holding hands and I smile.

Two boys with bikes cut between us. It takes us five minutes to get through all the people and back to the edge of the party where I said bye to Seymour. It's not like I expected him to still be waiting there, but I'm disappointed anyway.

Lana tugs on my hand. "Come on, let's go find him."

"You spent all this time trying to get to this party, and you're leaving already?" says a voice behind me.

Both Lana and I turn around slowly. He's holding a beef patty in one hand and the gas canister in the other.

"Ryde guy," she says.

"Sassy best friend," he says.

At some point I'm going to need to introduce them officially. But not right now.

Lana squeezes my hand. "I'll be with Tristán," she says, and takes off.

"Why are you leaving?" he asks. "Things go bad with Derrick?"

I shake my head. "Things went fine."

"Then how come you're –"

"I was trying to find you," I say.

"You forget something in my car?"

Man, he's going to make me spell it out for him. "You remember that hypothetical question you asked me before?"

His eyebrows climb his forehead and a bright, happy smile spreads across his face like sunshine.

He steps closer to me so there's about a foot of space between us. "So you finally have an answer for my hypothetical?" he asks.

"I do," I say, closing the distance between us.

The lights come back, and all around us, everyone cheers.

ACKNOWLEDGMENTS

DHONIELLE CLAYTON

This book was born during the COVID-19 pandemic. The world paused and we all felt like we were in a metaphorical blackout, fumbling around in the dark, trying to make sense of everything happening around us. But out of the chaos came this light, this beautiful little love, our novel. I am grateful for this tether of creativity when death and uncertainty swirled around me.

First, I'd like to thank my niece, Riley Clayton, who inspired the entire idea. If it weren't for our marathon movie-watching/ TV-binging, and you asking me why Black girls didn't get big love stories, this book wouldn't exist. Thanks for giving your aunt a challenge. I hope I continue to rise and meet every one of them. I love you, kid. You are one of my heart chambers.

To my ladies: Tiffany D. Jackson, Angie Thomas, Nic Stone, Ashley Woodfolk, and Nicola Yoon, you made my dreams come true. Thank you for your trust, for your hearts, for your time, for your talent, and for your willingness to jump headfirst into the dark with me. We made beautiful light together. It will see me through for a long, long time. This experience has been the highlight of my career. I am so happy to be leaving behind this book in the world with you all.

To Molly Ker Hawn: Thank you for being a dream maker with a lion heart. Your leadership, your wisdom, and your spirit helped make sure this book found its place. Thank you for taking such great care of me – of us.

To Mary Pender: You are the best partner in crime. Thank you for all that you do. You are a magic maker!

To Rosemary Brosnan: This editorial experience has been so amazing. You pushed me and made me dig deep. My writing has been transformed by your touch and wisdom. Thank you for the push.

To the Harper team: Suzanne Murphy, Erin Fitzsimmons, Courtney Stevenson, Ebony LaDelle, Patty Rosati, Audrey Diestelkamp, and team. Thank you for all that you've done for this book. It takes an army to launch a book, and I'm so happy to have this squad behind us.

To Mom and Dad: Thank you for the endless support, the wisdom, the food, the care. You listen to every complaint, soothe every wound, and breathe life into every dream. I wouldn't be *me* if you weren't *you*. I'm forever grateful to have witnessed your love for each other (and felt your love for me) so that I may write love into my work.

To the superhero librarians of the New York Public Library – Louise Lareau, Jenny Rosenoff, and Sue Yee: Thank you for your detailed insight, which helped make this story as accurate as it can be. You are the titans of our society. I feel proud to be one of you. I know the Children's Center moved right as this book was being written, and I appreciate your help in making this dreamy little love story work despite that. Thanks for the troubleshooting.

To the readers: Thank you for the support and I hope you keep your heart open to receive all the love the universe has in store for you.

TIFFANY D. JACKSON

I'd like to thank the captain of our ship, Dhonielle, for ~~forcing~~ convincing me to do this, even when I said this wasn't my lane. You always manage to help me believe in myself. To the Squad, I'm sorry for my "bright" idea to split up my story, which of course created more work for us all, but it came together beautifully. To Rosemary Brosnan, I'm sure it took a lot to wrangle us all, but you did it effortlessly, like a true Queen. To Molly Ker Hawn and Mary Pender, thanks for all that you do and continue to do. To my family, I love you. To that heffa COVID, you brought us together, but I'm fighting you on sight. And to NYC, you will always be my first love.

NIC STONE

First, to Dhonielle Clayton: Thank you for coming up with this harebrained idea and inviting me along for the ride. You da best. The Mollies: Molly Ker Hawn and Mollie Glick: Obviously agents with your name get s*** DONE. To Rosemary Brosnan: Thank you for taking a chance on us with this thing, and for whipping it into shape. To Jay Coles, Terry J. Benton-Walker, and Julian Winters: Your insights into this very much *not* #OwnVoice story (for me) were utterly invaluable, and I appreciate you all more than I could ever express. Pete Forester: Shout-out to you for helping my Southern ass get the NYC stuff right. To Nigel Livingstone: Again, you created the space and time for me to work. Even in the thick of a global pandemic. And to Michael Bonner: Much appreciation for allowing me to turn your delightfully quiet living room into my kid-free office so I could get this joint written. Love you all!

ANGIE THOMAS

God, thank you for getting me through 2020, and thank you for the bright spot that was working on this book during that roller coaster of a year.

Dhonielle the queen, thank you for lovingly dragging me into this and challenging my drama-loving self to write a love story. It's an honor to be a part of something so special. To the ladies, I'm so happy to create this beautiful book with you. Because of us, Black kids will know that they deserve the biggest love stories too. To Molly Ker Hawn and Mary Pender, thanks for being our rocks on this journey and making sure this book was taken care of. Rosemary Brosnan, thank you for making us dig deep to ensure this story is the best it can be. To the amazing Harper team, thank you for holding us down. To my mom, Julia, you're the real MVP. And to the readers: I hope you find the love you deserve. Your own story awaits.

ASHLEY WOODFOLK

Writing a book like this one was a dream come true. I got to work with some of my closest writer friends on a book unlike any I've ever read, but that is somehow also something I've been passively looking and longing for, for years. It wouldn't have been possible without Dhonielle roping us all into it, and I'll forever cherish the hours of brainstorming, the group text chain where we chatted about book stuff but also, literally everything else. So thanks to D (and the rest of the Blackout Bunch) for going on this adventure and inviting me along. Big thanks to my agent, Beth, for fielding millions of questions and answering all my panicky texts, and to our fearless leader, Molly Ker Hawn, who none of this would have been possible without. Thank you to Rosemary Brosnan for seeing something special in each of our stories, and working to shape them while appreciating and celebrating their differences. This book was a light in the middle of a very dark year, one that felt a bit like a blackout in lots of ways, and I'll be forever grateful to have been a part of its revolutionary joy.

NICOLA YOON

In the history of years, 2020 was the absolute longest. Still, there were bright spots, and getting to write this book with five of the most talented and fearless authors working was one of them. Thanks so much to Angie, Ashley, Dhonielle, Nic, and Tiffany for all their brilliance and imagination. Extra, extra special thanks to our fearless leader, Dhonielle, for roping us all into this project with her incredible idea. Her passion and dedication are boundless. Thanks to our wonderful editor, Rosemary Brosnan, for whipping our stories into shape, and to super agents Molly Ker Hawn and Mary Pender for whipping our deals into shape. Huge thanks to my indefatigable agent, Jodi Reamer, for always knowing all the things. And, of course, thanks to the loves of my life, David and Penny, just for being. You guys are always my brightest spots.

READ ON FOR
EXCLUSIVE CONTENT
FROM ALL
SIX AUTHORS!

DEAR READER,

Turn the lights off, break out the flashlight or light a candle, and come on this love adventure with us.

Let me tell you how this all began ...

When the world shut down during the height of the COVID-19 pandemic, we were all struggling to make sense of everything around us. Writing schedules halted. Our school visits were canceled. Festivals were in limbo. We found ourselves on pause from everything we used to do.

I live in Harlem, New York, and during quarantine, it seemed as if the entire city had paused and no one knew what to do or how to feel. The city felt like the lights had gone out ... just like in the book.

In order to find some sense of happiness, I'd been spending a lot of time hanging out with my fourteen-year-old niece and binging lots of teen shows and movies. She'd complained about the lack of Black kids getting big love stories in these films and shows, and I thought, *Wouldn't it be amazing if my friends and I worked on putting some love into the world right now – a little light in the darkness?*

Since everyone's schedules had been flipped upside down, I pitched the idea to five of my very close friends, who happen to be wonderful YA writers ☺. I'm lucky they all said yes and jumped in with their whole hearts to write this interconnected novel before even knowing if it would work or if we could sell it. They stepped out on faith and love because we knew it was so important.

We each picked an area of the city and a fun romance trope to explore in our stories. You'll find something for everyone . . . insta-love, enemies-to-lovers, exes-to-friends, love triangles, friends-to-lovers, and more. There's no one way to experience love.

We believe that Black teens deserve all different kinds of books, including ones about police brutality and systemic racism, but also about love and joy and magic. My worry is that when Black teens get only one type of book, they begin to believe that that is their story. The only one. They will always be the perpetually sassy sidekick or the angry kid or the victim or a teachable lesson for non-Black kids. I believe Black readers deserve a smorgasbord of options, just like other kids, and that they especially deserve the biggest love stories.

Keep your heart open. And always remember, even love stories can glow when the lights go out.

All the love,

Dhonielle Clayton

SURVIVAL GUIDE

DHONIELLE'S BLACKOUT SURVIVAL GUIDE

Food: Mini marshmallows. I'm obsessed with them right now. They're the perfect bite-sized sugar surge.

Book: Anne Rice's Vampire Chronicles. Might as well start over by candlelight.

Music: D'Angelo's *Black Messiah*. Time to chill out in the dark and keep calm. D'Angelo always provides.

Clothes: Flip-flops, fresh undies, and comfy pants.

Something useful: Backup phone charger and deodorant. It's going to be a long night, and I'll need to stay fresh and charged up.

Wild card item: Portable fan.

TIFFANY'S BLACKOUT SURVIVAL GUIDE

Food: Chocolate chip cookies. Because I am made of 75 percent cookie dough.

Book: Twilight series. They soothe me.

Music: A soca/afro-beat playlist. When the lights go out, it's time to party!

Clothes: Shorts, a tank top, and some flip-flops. I want to be as cool and comfortable as possible.

Something useful: My zombie apocalypse kit (at this point, if you don't have one, you can't be on my *Walking Dead* team).

Wild card item: A gas can. See above.

N/C'S BLACKOUT SURVIVAL GUIDE

Food: Some bougie self-made "trail mix" that includes dried mandarins, shelled pistachios, baked Parmesan crisps, candied pecans, chocolate-covered dried cherries, and freeze-dried raspberries. Delish!

Book: *The Color Purple* by Alice Walker.

Music: Hip-hop heavy playlist that includes a lot of Future, Migos, Drake, Travis Scott, Saweetie, DaBaby, and Megan Thee Stallion.

Clothes: Gotta have layers!

Something useful: Half-gallon canteen of water.

Wild card item: Perfume. Gotta smell good, even in the dark.

ANGIE'S BLACKOUT SURVIVAL GUIDE

Food: Protein shake. Boring, I know, but it'll keep me full, and I'm trying to survive, right?

Book: Anything fantasy. I'll need an escape.

Music: I'm a '90s kid through and through, so give me all of the '90s hip-hop: 2Pac, TLC, etc.

Clothes: Sweats or shorts and T-shirts, depending on the weather. I need to be comfortable. Oh, and sneakers, obviously.

Something useful: A first aid kit, and my laptop so I can still get some writing done.

Wild card item: A fully charged Nintendo Switch so I can play *Animal Crossing* while I wait.

ASHLEY'S BLACKOUT SURVIVAL GUIDE

Food: My go-to snack in any situation, but especially a stressful one, is Oatmeal Creme Pies. So having a couple of those stashed close by would be ideal in a blackout. A close second would be some Everything Pretzel Chips, preferably with spicy hummus to dip them in. To drink, I'd probably want some strawberry soda or Arizona Mucho Mango.

Book: I'd love to have some summery love stories to pass the time with, so *Now That I've Found You* by Kristina Forest, *Rise To The Sun* by Leah Johnson, or Jenny Han's The Summer I Turned Pretty series.

Music: *Kings of Summer* by ayokay is my favorite summer anthem (something about EDM feels summerish to me), or Arlo Parks's album *Collapsed in Sunbeams*.

Clothes: I'd hope I was wearing something cool, like a maxi dress with thin straps.

Something useful: A water bottle! Gotta stay hydrated.

Wild card item: My purse. Which is a New York–sized purse. Which is essentially a giant bag that would have *everything* else I'd need in it.

NICOLA'S BLACKOUT SURVIVAL GUIDE

Food: Jamaican beef patty with coco bread. It's the perfect food: delicious and nutritious, and you can eat it with just one hand.

Book: *The Norton Anthology of Poetry*, 5th edition. Not only is the book inspiring because of all the beautiful poetry, but the book itself is heavy and huge and can be used to whack someone over the head if necessary.

Music: *Love* by Kendrick Lamar and *Videotape* by Radiohead, because they are two of the most perfect songs ever written.

Clothes: A summer dress (preferably floral) for keeping cool and comfy sandals in case there's a lot of walking to be done.

Something useful: *The Norton Anthology of Poetry* for the same reasons as above!

Wild card item: Lego because it's the single greatest toy in the world.

Q&A

DHONIELLE CLAYTON

Which do you think is the more magical part of a love story: the what-if or the happy ending?

The most magical part of a love story has to be the happy ending . . . the what-if can disappear so quickly, but the promise of the love story is paramount. I come to a love story or romantic film waiting for the happily ever after to be delivered. Sometimes the what-if can turn into a no, and that disappointment is so heart-wrenching. Give me *all* the happy endings to all the love stories.

What do you think is the best book?

Ha! Now I must answer the same question I posed in my own story . . . which is an impossible question. I wouldn't have been able to complete the bet in my story because the choice of best book ebbs and flows for me. When I was a little girl, it was *Harriet the Spy* by Louise Fitzhugh or *The Phantom Tollbooth* by Norton Juster, and as a teen, it was the Dark Tower series by Stephen King, and now, as an adult who still very much feels like a teen reader, I'd have to go with *Passing* by Nella

Larsen. It's the book that reminds me why I love books and why I wanted to become a writer.

Was your story inspired by any relationships in your own life?
This is the ultimate secret, isn't it? – whether or not someone has a close friend that they're secretly in love with? Hehe. I'll never tell. But yes, much of my writing is inspired by my real life.

What are your favorite summertime love stories?
Southside with You, which is the story of how President Barack Obama and Michelle Obama met and fell in love.

What's the most romantic thing that happened to you as a teenager?
A very nice young man from a rival high school made me a mixtape and taped it to my car window during the school day, along with a letter and flowers. I was so embarrassed and shy and immature about all things love, but it was the most romantic gesture ever. Thanks, Joey. Teen me was the worst.

What is it about the lights going out that feels so magical?
Candles in the windows, flashlights, headlights, the moon … the darkness can create such a gorgeous atmosphere that is ripe for magic. So many people are afraid of the dark, but for me, the darkness has always felt like a place where things could blossom and be both frightening and electrifying. So in a city

as special as New York, much of its magic comes alive when the sun goes down.

Is there a particular rom-com trope that makes you swoon?
I'm a sucker for a good enemies-to-lovers rom-com trope. It feels like what my own love story in real life will probably be. I love the chaos that comes from the hatred softening over time, and how the two lovers end up surrendering to it. So satisfying.

Why does New York City inspire so many love stories?
New York City is a special place: millions of people, millions of potential meet-cutes, millions of possible love stories. I think the intense energy inspires creativity, love, and one-of-a-kind experiences. It isn't the most beautiful or romantic city in the world – that award goes to Paris, hands down, fight me – but there's something magical in all the skyscrapers and the tidal energy of this city that's conducive to a great big love story.

What was your favorite part of collaborating with Team Blackout?
The best part of collaborating with Team Blackout was the fact that each of these talented women jumped headfirst into the dark with me. I loved having five brilliant brains to navigate this wildly ambitious love story. I am grateful to get to publish with them. My work is made better by their insights, support, and trust.

TIFFANY D. JACKSON

What was your process for writing a story in pieces that ties the novel together?

I'm a super visual person – blame my film background. So when Dhonielle proposed this project and gave movie examples, the only way I saw the story coming together was telling it throughout the day, cutting and interlinking it much like a *Love Actually*. And selfishly, I wanted to see my characters experience the very moment the lights went out and have them feel the magic when they came back on.

In the spectrum of strong emotions that Kareem and Tammi experience, where does anger end and lingering love begin?

Anger ends with communication and forgiveness, since so much can be lost in the unsaid. Love begins again with acceptance and really seeing a person for who they are, not who you think they should be. If kids walk away from this book with at least that understanding of the foundation of love, I'd feel like I've done my job.

Was your story inspired by any relationships in your own life?

Most of my family lived through the 1970s New York City blackout and they all had different stories of the fear and panic that melted into the city on that insanely hot summer day. Whenever incidents erupt in New York City, everyone's first instinct is to get home, by any means necessary.

So when I think of Kareem and Tammi determined to make it back to Brooklyn, I picture my family doing the same.

What are your favorite summertime love stories?
Of course, *Dirty Dancing* reigns supreme! I remember being a kid, wishing I'd run into my own Patrick Swayze at dance school. Next, *The Notebook*. Forbidden love with a boy from the other side of the tracks who'd risk anything to be with you? Swoon! I watched it a zillion times. Ice-cream dates became a mandatory requirement ever since.

What's the most romantic thing that happened to you as a teenager?
I slow-danced with my crush to *Always and Forever* by Heatwave. I swore it would be our wedding song and I can't even remember the boy's name. Hahahaha!

What is it about the lights going out that feels so magical?
I have absolutely no idea. But if I did, I'd bottle up that magic and give it to every broken-hearted girl around the world. We all deserve to believe in fairy tales.

Is there a particular rom-com trope that makes you swoon?
Enemies to lovers has always been my jam.

Why does New York City inspire so many love stories?
You know the "If you can make it here you can make it

anywhere" cliché? There's something to that. Because when you find your person – that needle in the haystack in a city of millions – it's literally unforgettable magic that you have to share with the world.

What was your favorite part of collaborating with Team Blackout?
My favorite part was the collaboration itself. It was a complete team effort. We all supported each other and played to our strengths. It's amazing seeing six powerful Black women change the game.

NIC STONE

Do you think wearing masks – literal or metaphorical – makes it easier for people to fall in love, or harder?
I think most people fall in love with masks on, but in order to stay in love for real, you have to take them off.

Why is it so hard for JJ (or anyone) to tell himself honest stories about who he is? What is it about the darkness that brings those truths out?
I think we're all handed role narratives we're "supposed to fit" in order to be acceptable, and not fitting them feels dire to most people. So we lie and try to force ourselves into spaces that aren't meant for us. In the dark, there are no distractions and all of our other senses are heightened, so we're typically faced with full awareness of ourselves and what's inside us.

Was your story inspired by any relationships in your own life?
Nope! I prefer to explore experiences I *haven't* lived.

What are your favorite summertime love stories?
I don't think I actually have any?

What's the most romantic thing that happened to you as a teenager?
The guy who wound up being my senior prom date was a visual artist, and he "prom-posed" by creating this massive poster (like I had to lay it out on the floor) with a drawing of him asking me to prom, and a drawing of me with an empty speech bubble to write my answer in. Totally should've dated *that* guy instead of the awful one I picked instead.

What is it about the lights going out that feels so magical?
Depends on the circumstances. Sometimes the lights going out is terrifying. But if you're with the right people, it can be a space/opportunity for open discussion without scrutiny. There's something disarming about being in the dark with another person – especially one you love.

Is there a particular rom-com trope that makes you swoon?
I personally love the combo of enemies-to-forbidden-lovers. So much drama! Heightens the tension for sure.

Why does New York City inspire so many love stories?

I think it's the combination of movement and the sheer mass of people. Just makes you want to hold those you love that much closer.

What was your favorite part of collaborating with Team Blackout?

Putting the connective tissue into the stories. One of my characters is one of Tiff's characters' younger brother and the son of Angie's bus driver, the other one plays basketball with the brother of one of Dhonielle's characters, who is also the cousin to one of Angie's; one of my characters' grandpas lives where Ashley's characters meet . . . Creating these relationships and interconnecting the stories was so much fun and really highlighted the power of collaboration.

ANGIE THOMAS

How much of love (romantic or otherwise) is made up of paying attention, being "here-here"?

A lot of it, if not most. Attention is one of the most powerful love languages. It says that you care, that you're here, and that you're invested. It's the heartbeat of love.

When writing this story, did you always intend for Kayla to make the choice she does?

I did. Self-love is sometimes the best love, and by showing Kayla choosing herself, I hoped to show just how important that is. But I also wanted to show that it's okay if you don't have it all figured out just yet. At sixteen/seventeen, people rarely do. 😊

Was your story inspired by any relationships in your own life?
Not really. I've never been in a love triangle (or square?) before – haha. But I *have* chosen myself. 😊

What are your favorite summertime love stories?
I'm not sure it's summertime but one of my favorites is the movie *Brown Sugar*. Hip-hop + Black love = the perfect way to steal Angie's heart.

What's the most romantic thing that happened to you as a teenager?
I had no romance as a teen – haha.

What is it about the lights going out that feels so magical?
Because there's something quiet, peaceful, and intimate about the dark. It allows you to see new sides to a person that you wouldn't see in the light.

Is there a particular rom-com trope that makes you swoon?
Best friends turned lovers.

Why does New York City inspire so many love stories?
Because it's the city of endless possibilities.

What was your favorite part of collaborating with Team Blackout?

Finally getting to collaborate with some of my dear friends, who are also some of the most talented authors in the world. ☺

ASHLEY WOODFOLK

In your story, characters' love stories linger and play a role in the present. Do you think it's just as important to tell the stories of love that ended badly as it is to share stories of true love?

Absolutely. But also: just because a love story ends doesn't mean the love wasn't real or true. If you're lucky, you'll experience a few great loves over the course of your life. They won't always love you back. And most of them will come to an end. But I think each one helps shape you into the person you're meant to become, and sometimes the bad ones shape you even more than the ones that end well. If we only tell stories of people who stay together, we do our own growth and pasts a disservice. All relationships have value. If you let them, each one can teach you what you're looking for, what you're willing to compromise on, and what your deal-breakers are. And as you collect this information about yourself, you get closer and closer to finding the relationship that will be worth the work it takes to sustain it (and the person who is willing to work toward creating a healthy partnership where you're each getting what you need).

Are you team "different can work" or team "we just fit" when it comes to relationships? (Or both?)

I think every relationship is unique. There's real value in finding someone you just vibe with. There's also so much to be said for two people who decide they love each other and do everything they can to make it work despite their differences. Both can also exist simultaneously. For example, my husband and I are polar opposites when it comes to our taste in music, TV, clothes, etc. But we like to do the same things and our values match up in an ideal way. So I'm team "whatever works for you".

Was your story inspired by any relationships in your own life?

Mine was inspired by all the girls I've had crushes on over the years but never had the courage to act on.

What are your favorite summertime love stories?

I love *Call Me By Your Name*. As for movies, *Dirty Dancing*, *Adventureland*, and *(500) Days of Summer* immediately come to mind.

What's the most romantic thing that happened to you as a teenager?

My tenth grade boyfriend and I had broken up, but he still came with me to a dance because we were trying really hard to "be friends". We'd been flirting since he picked me up but still clinging to the "just friends" thing for whatever reason, until the last dance of the night. It was a slow dance, and he leaned forward and whispered into my ear, "You know I still want you, right?" I can't remember if we kissed then or later, but we instantly knew we were getting back together.

What is it about the lights going out that feels so magical?
Whenever something unexpected happens, it always feels like anything is possible.

Is there a particular rom-com trope that makes you swoon?
There's only one bed. Because of course there's only one bed. And we all know what's going to happen when they both have to share that bed . . . They're gonna fall in looooove.

Why does New York City inspire so many love stories?
New York City is a big place that sometimes feels impossibly small. You bump into the same people despite there being literally millions of strangers. It's a microcosm of the whole world. It's a place where serendipity seems impossible to avoid. And serendipitous meetings are the beginning of so many love stories.

What was your favorite part of collaborating with Team Blackout?
Knowing we all want the same thing: for Black kids to have love stories that center and celebrate their unique beauty.

NICOLA YOON

Okay, but what's your take on the Ship of Theseus??

I think the answer doesn't really matter. It's the asking of the question that counts.

What sorts of situations make for the best meet-cutes?

Anything where the characters are out of their comfort zones and forced to be together. Falling in love is as much about self-discovery as it is about discovering the other person.

Was your story inspired by any relationships in your own life?

All my love stories are inspired by my relationship with my husband. He's my best friend and we spend a lot of time talking about big philosophical ideas like the Ship of Theseus.

What are your favorite summertime love stories?

I'm not sure if these are summertime, but some of my recent favorites are *Red, White & Royal Blue* by Casey McQuiston and *Act Your Age, Eve Brown* by Talia Hibbert.

What's the most romantic thing that happened to you as a teenager?

Absolutely nothing romantic happened to me as a teenager! I was shy and awkward and a huge nerd. I'm a perennial late bloomer. All the romance came later.

What is it about the lights going out that feels so magical?
The world is so mysterious in the dark. I think that feeling of mystery inspires a sense of adventure and possibility.

Is there a particular rom-com trope that makes you swoon?
Enemies to lovers! I love witty banter between smart characters. Also, there's nothing better than the moment the characters realize they should stop fighting and start kissing.

Why does New York City inspire so many love stories?
New York City is a universe unto itself. You can find every kind of person and every kind of story there.

What was your favorite part of collaborating with Team Blackout?
The group chat, which was just so funny all the time! Kidding aside, my favorite part was just getting to work with these amazingly talented women. 2020 was a hard year, but writing these love stories starring Black kids with my friends and professional heroes made the year a little easier.